**THE CAT
WHO
SAVED
THE
LIBRARY**

Without limiting the exclusive rights of any author, contributor or the publisher of this publication, any unauthorized use of this publication to train generative artificial intelligence (AI) technologies is expressly prohibited. HarperCollins also exercise their rights under Article 4(3) of the Digital Single Market Directive 2019/790 and expressly reserve this publication from the text and data mining exception.

This is a work of fiction. Names, characters, places, and incidents are products of the author's imagination or are used fictitiously and are not to be construed as real. Any resemblance to actual events, locales, organizations, or persons, living or dead, is entirely coincidental.

THE CAT WHO SAVED THE LIBRARY. Copyright © 2024 by Sosuke Natsukawa. English Translation Copyright © 2025 by Louise Heal Kawai. "A Note from the Cover Designer" by Stephen Brayda copyright © 2025 by HarperCollins Publishers. All rights reserved. No part of this book may be used or reproduced in any manner whatsoever without written permission except in the case of brief quotations embodied in critical articles and reviews. For information, address HarperCollins Publishers, 195 Broadway, New York, NY 10007. In Europe, HarperCollins Publishers, Macken House, 39/40 Mayor Street Upper, Dublin 1, D01 C9W8, Ireland.

HarperCollins books may be purchased for educational, business, or sales promotional use. For information, please email the Special Markets Department at SPsales@harpercollins.com.

Originally published as 君を守ろうとする猫の話 in Japan in 2024 by Shogakukan Inc.

harpercollins.com

FIRST HARPERVIA PAPERBACK PUBLISHED IN 2026

Designed by Yvonne Chan

Library of Congress Cataloging-in-Publication Data is available upon request.

ISBN 978-0-06-341925-4

Printed in the United States of America

26 27 28 29 30 LBC 5 4 3 2 1

CONTENTS

How It All Began
1

The One Who Walks Beside Us
13

The One Who Was Created
55

The One Who Proliferates
111

The One Who Questions
171

How It All Ended
199

A Note from the Cover Designer
209

About the Author
211

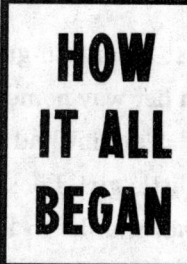

HOW IT ALL BEGAN

Recently books had been disappearing. Or at least that's what it looked like.

Nanami folded her skinny arms and stared at the bookshelves in front of her. She mulled over the evidence. Books were apparently vanishing from the library.

Her use of the phrases "looked like" and "apparently" was because it was hard to prove. This old library had a huge collection of books. And as the primary job of a library wasn't to keep all the books neat and dust-free on the shelves, but to lend out as many to the public as possible, obviously not all of the books were there all of the time. If Nanami had been a librarian, she could have checked the books' lending history, or if she'd been a brilliant detective, she might have been able to solve the mystery by her powers of deduction but, unfortunately, she was just an eighth-grade student who liked to drop by the library on her way home from school.

Nanami had been visiting this library ever since she was a little girl. Back then it was her father who used to bring her and, thanks to him, she had gotten into the habit of coming every single day. This meant that she was very familiar with the arrangement of books and had immediately spotted that something was different. When it came to her beloved library, she was confident that her memory was at least more accurate than the head librarian's and possibly even more brilliant than a detective's.

The first thing that had caught her attention were the gaps here and there on the shelves. After a while she realized that those spaces were never refilled—they remained gaps for as long as she had been checking them. Robert Louis Stevenson's *Treasure Island* was missing from the children's fiction section. The beautiful white-spined copy of *Anne of Green Gables* and the adventure story of Captain Nemo and his *Twenty Thousand Leagues Under the Sea* were also never returned.

Over in the picture book section, two of Nanami's favorites, *Mr. Owl* and *Frederick*, were nowhere to be seen.

A stroll by the literary fiction shelves revealed that both Hesse's *Beneath the Wheel* and Hemingway's *The Old Man and the Sea* were gone.

In fact, on every shelf throughout the library were empty spaces that hadn't been there before.

Nanami had wondered for a moment whether people had just started borrowing more books, then she swiftly dismissed that thought. This was a large-scale library with an extensive collection of books, but it was no modern state-of-the-art facility. The building itself was dilapidated; the air-conditioning barely worked; there were dark corners where the light bulbs had burned out; and here and there a musty smell assaulted your nose. In other words, there was no reason for the number of users to increase. And it was clear just from looking that the library's spacious aisles were as deserted as ever.

What struck Nanami as curious was that none of the adults in the library seemed to have spotted anything. The staff were always too occupied with paperwork to have noticed any changes in their environment.

"What's going on?" Nanami mused out loud. Of course, just because she'd dared to ask the question aloud didn't mean that she'd get an answer. She stood still in one central spot and swiveled slowly around to scan the whole floor. From a distance, the tall metal shelves seemed to be as tightly packed as ever, but when she walked along the aisles, she saw the gaps here and there like pulled teeth. Perhaps it was because Nanami was so familiar with the library that she noticed this phenomenon, to her the changes were undeniable.

The books were definitely gone.

"You're saying I need to check on the books?"

The voice of elderly Mr. Hamura, the librarian at the main

reception desk, wasn't all that loud, but as the first floor had a high vaulted ceiling, his words reverberated through the whole library. Still, with so few patrons it wasn't as if anyone was there to hear it. Just one older woman who happened to be passing by threw Nanami and Mr. Hamura a quick glance.

Nanami tried to keep her tone as casual as possible.

"Yeah, some books are missing that should be there. More than just one or two."

Mr. Hamura peered over his reading glasses at the young girl in the school uniform.

"I see. Well, that is a serious problem," he pronounced, before turning his attention back to the file on the desk in front of him. He hastily scribbled something down before continuing.

"If you're going to make a fuss every time you can't find the books you want on the shelves, then how are you going to be able to use a library?"

For a moment, Nanami looked confused at the librarian's logic, but she soon realized that it was the old man's eccentric sense of humor. He snapped the plastic file shut and looked up at the junior high schooler.

"Look, Nanami-chan," he said, stroking his spindly white beard, "this is a library. If anyone coming here wants to borrow a book, it's a very simple procedure. And that's why sometimes books are there and sometimes they're not. That procedure hasn't changed since the time you were in preschool and came here with your father to borrow a copy of *The Very Hungry Caterpillar*. And if you've forgotten, you're very welcome to check the terms of use up there on the wall."

It's just not my day, thought Nanami, sighing inwardly.

Old Mr. Hamura was more than just a librarian. He'd worked for decades in this library and had chosen to stay on at the reception desk even after retirement. You could call him a living encyclopedia of this ancient library. Although he was cynical, moody, and rather difficult, he wasn't a bad person. He had introduced Nanami to all kinds of wonderful books. However, when he was in one of his moods, you risked getting on the wrong end of his caustic tongue. Today was clearly one of those days.

"This library," the old man went on, emphasizing his words by tapping the cover of his file with a bony finger, "is as old as I am. And old people get worn out and forget things. Young people's job is to take care of the elderly and not to get caught up worrying about a few missing books."

How long is this going to drag on . . . ?

Nanami's mind had already wandered from this fruitless conversation at the first-floor reception desk up to the British Literature section on the second floor. She was probably going to finish her current read, *Wuthering Heights*, today or the following day, and she needed to choose her next book. Now was clearly not the best time to ask Mr. Hamura for a recommendation.

"Although I do appreciate your concern, I've got a lot of work to do—"

The librarian was interrupted by the sound of Nanami's cell phone chiming softly in her pocket. It wasn't a text message; it was her evening reminder alarm.

She promptly pulled an inhaler from her bag, put it to her mouth, and took a deep breath. Nanami needed this treatment for her asthma several times a day, but she tended to forget her evening dose. It was her father who had suggested she set this alarm.

Mr. Hamura waited for her to finish.

"I'll take a look at the shelves later," he said, in a somewhat gentler tone than before. "I'd rather you spend time taking care of yourself instead of worrying about books."

Naturally Nanami didn't tell the old man to mind his own business. She simply nodded her thanks and turned to leave. As she walked away, she let rip her parting shot, albeit inside her head.

Useless!

She was well aware that she had just insulted the living encyclopedia—the withered old man who, some might say, embodied this whole library.

Nanami Kosaki was a short and skinny thirteen-year-old girl in the second year of junior high school. She was very pale because asthma had always meant she had limited exposure to the outside world. Her asthma was a bit like a wild horse, and any kind of exercise or physical or mental stress would set it off galloping around her respiratory system on its iron hooves. Too many times during her elementary school years she'd been rushed by ambulance to the emergency room. Because of her illness, she'd never experienced the joy of playing outdoors with friends, running about in the fresh air, and she had become used to spending time alone in the library after school. Many people sympathized with her plight, but Nanami didn't feel disadvantaged at all. As long as she had no asthma attacks, a place where she could absorb herself in books and be free to read as much as she liked was perfect. And this was why she took the mysterious disappearance of library books very seriously indeed.

"He told me to check the terms of use!"

Nanami was in the reading area on the second floor of the library, her head resting on a desk. She had a favorite among the large, well-worn desks. It was one by the window where the sunlight fell just right; it was the spot where she would sit and read after school. A book was open on the desk, but right now she felt too irritated to follow the words on the page.

"Me, I'm a regular here, and I take the trouble to tell him I'm worried about the books, and that stubborn old man . . ."

"What a nightmare. Well, good for you for trying."

The response came from the girl sitting across from her. Itsuka Imamura and Nanami Kosaki had been friends since they were little.

Itsuka was tall and carried herself well, making her look at least a school grade above the petite Nanami. She wore her hair in a neat, short-cropped style, a contrast to the long black hair that Nanami tied back in a ponytail.

Itsuka glanced down through the open space to the first-floor reception area and gave a sympathetic laugh.

"Old Ham always looks so grumpy that it's impossible to tell if he's in a good mood or a bad one," she remarked.

"Today was really bad. Seems he was busy or something. I misread him completely."

Nanami lifted her head and rested her chin on her hand.

"Old Ham" was the nickname that Itsuka had given Mr. Hamura. Nanami thought it suited the librarian perfectly with his tough old wrinkly face.

"Are there really books going missing?" added Itsuka, scanning the bookshelves in the vicinity. "It looks to me as if the place is full of them."

Across a narrow aisle from the reading corner were rows of plain steel bookcases. At the end of each case was a label indicating the contents—Japanese Literature, Economics, Philosophy, History, Folklore—giving a sense of a vast and varied collection of books lining the shelves. Beyond those bookshelves, not visible from their current location in the reading corner, were more sections organized by country of origin, containing meticulously arranged shelves of literature from all around the world. From the girls' viewpoint in the sunny reading corner, the long rows of towering bookcases stretching into the gloomy half darkness was a magnificent sight.

"With all those books, how can you even tell that any are missing?"

"Well, there aren't any new releases or bestsellers missing, so probably most people wouldn't even notice," Nanami explained. "But plenty of older books that were borrowed a long time ago—*Gauche the Cellist* as well as *Knight's Fee*—have never been returned."

"So only people like you, who practically live around here, would ever notice?"

"You're saying I hang out here too much?"

"Well, you've spotted what's going on, and Old Ham has no idea, so that's proof that he's no more than a kind of landlord around here. You're like a proper tenant."

The two girls were really close and teased each other this way all the time. Their houses were right in the same neighborhood, and they'd gone to the same elementary school. Now that they were in junior high, Itsuka had joined the archery club, which met before and after school. Because of this, the two no longer walked to and from school together. However, on the days she had no club activity, Itsuka would turn up at the library with her archery bow wrapped up in a black cloth. She was devoted to practicing her draw at home and was a highly respected member of the archery club, popular with older and younger students alike.

"Why would books just disappear like that?" Itsuka asked. "Even if someone's stealing them, in the end they're no more than battered old used books. You'd get nothing if you tried to sell them online."

"I've no idea," replied Nanami, "but . . ."

She stopped and looked around a moment, dropping her voice to a whisper.

"I've seen this really shady-looking guy in here."

Itsuka's expression changed and she followed Nanami's

gaze around the reading corner, but there wasn't another soul at any of the desks. A little farther away an elderly woman sat in a seat by the window, staring vaguely outside, and in the picture book corner they saw a mother with a baby stroller. Needless to say, there weren't any shady-looking characters hanging around.

"Are you really sure he was shady?"

"I can't say yet, but I know that I've seen this one really freaky guy hanging about. I haven't said anything to Old Ham yet though."

"Well, you'll have to be careful how you bring that up. If you pick the wrong moment, he'll flip out at you."

"Deep down he's not so bad. He's always suggesting good books to me."

"Is that one of them?"

Itsuka looked down at the book Nanami was reading. Nanami nodded.

"It's *Wuthering Heights* by Emily Brontë. One of his top recommendations."

"Really? It's so thick and the font is so tiny. Is it any good?"

"It's really interesting. They call it a love story, but it's so much more than that. It's about this man who is really poor when he's young and is bullied by this rich man. Anyway, he becomes rich himself and comes back to get his revenge. Old Ham said it was one of the greatest revenge stories in literary history."

"The world of literature sounds really dark," said Itsuka, frowning.

The old woman who'd been staring out of the window picked

up her walking stick and began to make her way toward the elevator. Itsuka got up too.

"I'd better get going," she said.

"Aren't you going to do your homework first?" asked Nanami.

"My parents are both working late so I've got to get dinner for my little brother. I got a text earlier."

"Ah, it sucks that they're always so busy."

"Yeah, I guess," said Itsuka lightly, grabbing her archery bow, which was propped up against the wall. "But I know it must be worse for you."

Itsuka had a point. Nanami's mother had passed away when she was still young, and Nanami lived alone with her father. It was a sign of how close the two girls were that they could speak so matter-of-factly about this.

"I can't imagine what it would be like if there was just me and my father," Itsuka added.

"It's not bad at all," Nanami replied. "When Dad's busy he eats out, so I just have to make my own meals. And if I don't feel like cooking, I stop by the bento shop."

"You're always so upbeat about things."

When Nanami was in elementary school, her father used to come home early to make dinner; by the time she was in junior high, he'd gotten busier at work, and now he regularly got home late.

"Being an only child might be easier," Itsuka sighed. "At my house, if my mother works late two or three days in a row, the house ends up a total mess. My brother is useless—all he does is eat, and he never cleans up after himself."

Nanami laughed, although she couldn't help feeling a twinge of envy. It was truly hard on Itsuka that she had to prepare meals, but at least she got to sit down at a table and eat with her brother. In Nanami's case, whenever her father was late, she had to eat alone.

"See you later!"

Itsuka had already started walking away. Suddenly she stopped and turned back to Nanami.

"Now don't go getting mixed up in anything too crazy, okay?" she warned her friend. "You're not strong enough."

And with that she raised her bow in a parting gesture and strode away.

Nanami was happy to have a friend like Itsuka who would talk to her so frankly.

In elementary school she'd been in and out of the hospital because of her asthma and, to make matters worse, the fact that she had no mother meant that she had been bombarded by exaggerated expressions of sympathy both at school and in the hospital. She truly appreciated a friend like Itsuka who would simply say "Hi" or "Hey there" to her and treat her like a regular person.

I should invite her to dinner sometime, she mused. She wasn't sure how her father would feel about two junior high schoolers eating dinner together, but Nanami thought it was a great idea.

She turned her attention back to *Wuthering Heights*. Heathcliff's revenge was about to reach its climax.

THE ONE WHO WALKS BESIDE US

Nanami was absorbed in her book and barely noticed the reddish glow that had crept across her reading desk. When she finally looked up, she saw the sun was low, tinting the sky over the roofs of the houses. The air by the window was cooling off rapidly.

It seemed only a few days ago that the trees lining the streets had taken on their autumn colors; now it already felt on the verge of winter. Sunny days were pleasant; then, once the sun began to set, the temperature would plummet. Nanami didn't mind the cold itself, but the dry air of winter was a nightmare for an asthma sufferer. It didn't really matter if the weather was hot or cold, her activity was always restricted anyway. After switching to the school winter uniform, she would just add a coat or a scarf as the season progressed.

Wuthering Heights had reached its dramatic conclusion, and she realized now that she had been reading for a long time. As she watched the lengthening shadows of the trees, she heard children's voices coming from the elementary school playground next door. Even in the twilight she could make out a group of boys chasing after a soccer ball.

That late already...

The sun shone into the library at a deep, almost horizontal angle, and there wasn't a soul to be seen. Both the old woman at the window seat and the mother in the picture book section were long gone. But it wasn't unusual for the place to be deserted.

Nanami checked the clock and saw that it was almost six o'clock—closing time. She shut her copy of *Wuthering Heights* and put it away in her bag. It was as she turned to leave that she noticed a man standing in front of one of the bookshelves a short distance away. The man was solidly built and dressed in a gray suit. He had his back to Nanami, and although she couldn't see his face, a voice in her head shouted out an instinctive warning.

That's him!

She'd seen him here many times before. The perfect, wrinkle-free suit and the old-fashioned deerstalker peaked cap in the same shade of gray as the suit gave him the appearance of someone of higher rank than a regular salaryman. Although there was nothing particularly odd about his behavior, Nanami had noticed that it was invariably after his visits to the library that books would disappear. This was the shady-looking guy whom she had mentioned to Itsuka.

Of course, there was no proof that he was actually a book thief . . .

Nanami tried to calm her palpitating heart and growing sense of unease.

As the man disappeared behind the bookshelf, she got to her feet and silently walked over to where he'd been standing.

That particular shelf was filled with mystery novels aimed at YA readers, by authors such as Edogawa Ranpo and Arthur Conan Doyle. Nanami looked at the familiar titles and immediately spotted something. Right next to a row of the collected editions of Sherlock Holmes, there was a large empty space. It was where the complete set of *Arsène Lupin, Gentleman Thief* had been: the first ten volumes were gone. In other words, a third of the thirty-volume set was missing. This was the first time that she had seen so many books vanish at once. Never mind the sheer number of books, the man had some nerve taking these editions . . .

Maurice Leblanc's Lupin series was one of Nanami's favorites. The main character was a master of disguise and of martial arts, a thief who helped the poor and the suffering. When Nanami had been in elementary school, Lupin was a hero to her. She'd been so obsessed with these books that she used to get into trouble with her father for reading them in bed in the dark. She knew practically every word of *The Hollow Needle* and *813* by heart, she'd read them so many times.

Nanami looked in the direction the man had gone and saw him rounding the corner at the end of a long bookcase. And for a fleeting moment she also caught sight of a bulging black bag.

She began to walk faster.

There was a break in the rows of bookcases; Nanami stopped to peek through, and this time spotted the man entering the aisle marked French Literature. She crept after him and noticed a strange feeling deep in her chest. She frowned.

Sudden movements and exertion can trigger an asthma attack. The words of her doctor echoed in her ears. Overlapping this was a high-pitched whistling sound in the back of her throat, but Nanami didn't stop. By the time she reached the sign for French Literature on the end of the bookcase, the whistle had increased to a whine that filled her lungs.

"Oh no."

Her voice was already weak. A dangerous sign.

From her right pocket she pulled out her inhaler, leaning back against a bookcase to try to calm her ragged breathing. She mustn't panic. She carefully counted for ten seconds, during which she confirmed the attack wasn't getting any worse.

"I can't run around playing detective."

As soon as the words were out of her mouth she sank to the floor, her back still against the bookcase. Nanami didn't mind knowing that she couldn't run around in the woods like Huckleberry Finn or hike along train tracks like Gordie in *The Body* by Stephen King. Still, it would be a lie to say she didn't regret her inability to move at a crucial moment like this one.

"I'll just have to be as clever as Lupin," she muttered, half in complaint, but at the same time to bolster her resolve. Nanami knew there was no point in letting herself get discouraged over every small setback. Her airways might be sluggish, but her mind was knife-edge sharp. The crucial point was that books had been secretly removed from the library. A large portion of the Lupin collection was gone, so many volumes that this time even the stubborn old librarian wouldn't be able to snort with contempt.

Who was the mysterious man? And why would he steal old books from a library? Surely there was nothing he could gain from doing that.

As she thought this over, Nanami turned her head and peered down the aisle where she'd last seen the man, and let out an involuntary gasp.

Throughout the library building, the bookcases were all constructed the same—tall steel structures, identical narrow aisles stretching between them. The ceilings were all the same dreary gray, with dull fluorescent lights evenly spaced. Just because an aisle was filled with shelves of French literature didn't mean that it was decorated in the style of the Palais de Versailles . . .

Right now, what Nanami was seeing was not the familiar dimly lit aisle; nor was it a gorgeous example of baroque architecture. Instead, the far end of the aisle was infused with a soft bluish-white light. In the foreground were the familiar well-worn complete works of Baudelaire and Flaubert, but farther down, the shelves themselves seemed to have taken on a blue glow. What's more, the walls at the far end of the library had vanished and the bookshelves appeared to continue endlessly into the light.

"What's going on . . . ?" Nanami was stunned.

This library was like a garden to Nanami, a place she had roamed freely since she was a little girl. She'd even wandered into the office area and the storeroom and been scolded by Old Ham. But she'd never seen this glowing passageway before.

As if the light were drawing her in, she scrambled to her feet, but just at that moment she heard a deep, rich voice from behind her.

"Don't. Better stay away."

Nanami spun around. There was nobody there. Nothing. Well, nothing except for a small, round shadow huddled under the Italian Literature sign on the opposite side of the aisle.

From beneath two neat triangular ears gleamed a pair of jade-green eyes. Shining silver whiskers extended tidily on both sides.

"A cat . . . ?"

It was unmistakably a cat.

As if in response, the cat got to its feet and padded slowly over to Nanami. It was a big sturdy cat, its fur a mixture of orangey brown, yellow, and white. It walked right up to her, its beautiful eyes flashed, and then it opened its mouth. Once again she heard the deep, rich voice.

"Are you all right?"

Nanami was too shocked to reply.

"You looked as if you were struggling just now."

The sounds really did come from the cat's mouth. Although the words themselves showed concern for Nanami, the tone in which they were spoken was intimidating.

Nanami blinked a few times before giving a tentative nod.

"Yeah, I . . . er . . . think I'm okay."

"Splendid."

The cat gave a leisurely nod of its head, then turned to face the strange light.

"There's no point in trying so hard," it continued. "You can chase him but you'll never catch him."

It was such a deep, resounding voice that Nanami felt it in the pit of her stomach. As far as she was concerned, there was nothing wrong with a library and cat combination. It was just that when it came to talking cats, it was a whole other story.

She put her hand to her chest and took one deep breath. The noises that she'd heard earlier in her body seemed to have subsided. There was no asthma attack. She'd read in some book that when an attack got really bad, sometimes the brain didn't get enough oxygen, causing hallucinations. That wasn't the case right now. She turned her attention back to the talking animal in front of her.

"You're a cat, right?"

"Seriously? What do I look like? A dog?"

A cat was standing there asking a human being if it looked like a dog. It was pure chaos. There was absolutely nothing reassuring about its response.

"You see, none of the cats that I know talk," Nanami ventured.

"Well, that's a stupid thing to say," the cat declared. "We cats just don't babble on meaninglessly like humans do. We speak when we need to speak, and we are silent when we need to be silent. That's how cats are."

It was the first time Nanami had heard this definition of a cat. She put her hand to her forehead, even though she didn't have a headache. The cat continued calmly.

"Anyway, there's something I need to tell you. Stay away from that passageway."

"And what exactly *is* that passageway?"

"It's nothing."

"Well, it clearly isn't nothing."

Nanami wasn't going to let the cat's poor explanation pass without a challenge.

"However you look at it, there's nothing normal about that."

"Then let me put it another way—it's none of your business."

The harsh words were clearly intended to put her off.

"The problem is much trickier than you might think. If you don't tread carefully, then things can be really dangerous. Beyond this point—"

"You know something about that man, don't you?" Nanami interrupted.

The blunt question seemed to catch the cat off guard. It was the first time that Nanami saw it lose its cool. A hint of bewilderment crossed its features.

"Did he steal any books?" the cat asked Nanami.

"Yes, he did, but—"

"If you went to the end of that passageway, you'd find the books that he's taken. But listen, kid . . ."

The cat's voice grew stern.

"As I said just now, this isn't a matter that concerns you. What you need to do right now is very simple. You shut your mouth, block your ears, avert your eyes, and leave here right away. It'll be as if nothing ever happened . . . Aaagh!"

The cat cried out as Nanami reached out and grabbed it by the scruff of the neck. She brought the creature's face up close to her own.

"Wh-what are you doing?" it protested loudly.

"You said the books are down there?"

"Let me go! I'm telling you this for your own good!"

The cat tried to glare at Nanami. However, now that it was dangling from her hand it was nowhere near as authoritative as before. All it could do was wave its thick tail from side to side.

"Tell me how we can get the books back!" demanded Nanami.

"Didn't you hear me tell you it was dangerous?"

"So, if you say it's dangerous, that means there must be a way to get them back. Tell me!"

The cat gazed back at Nanami with an array of emotions in its expression—dismay, irritation, confusion, and more.

"And if I refuse?"

Nanami looked thoughtful.

"Then I'll keep on dangling you like this until my hands turn numb and I can't move them anymore."

"That's just ridiculous—"

"Try me! I may look weak but I'm stronger than you think. These arms have carried piles of heavy books over the years."

The cat stopped talking when it realized Nanami was serious.

After a moment of silence, it muttered in a resigned voice, "Put me down."

Nanami let go and the cat dropped to the floor and shook itself.

"You're a very strange girl," it remarked. "Aren't you afraid? The majority of human beings would run away screaming if a cat spoke to them."

"Then I'm in the minority."

"No, you're not. The rest of them would pretend not to hear."

Nanami found herself nodding.

"In my case, I was startled, but I wasn't scared," she said. "I was more concerned that something very precious had been stolen from me."

"Something precious?"

"The Lupin collection."

Even though Nanami continued to speak calmly, the cat must have spotted the earnest look in her eyes. It didn't make any more objections, instead keeping its gaze on the girl's face, its voice low and filled with curiosity.

"You're absolutely serious about this, aren't you?"

Nanami nodded. "Is a weak girl with asthma so useless?" she asked.

"Asthma isn't a problem, and it doesn't matter if you are a

girl or a boy. At the far end of that passageway, it's truth and the power of the heart that matter."

"I don't always understand complicated concepts, but if it's a matter of the heart, I might be able to help. I'm tougher than I look."

The cat stared at Nanami awhile longer before speaking.

"Somehow or other that appears to be true."

It took a deep breath and looked up at the girl.

"You really want to come with me?"

"Yes. If it means we can get the books back."

"I have no idea what's going to happen on this journey. So, kid, is that all right with you?"

Nanami nodded decisively.

"First," she said, lifting one of the cat's front paws with her left hand then squeezing it with her right, "don't call me 'kid.' My name is Nanami. Nice to meet you."

The cat recoiled slightly.

"I'm Tiger the Tabby," it replied grumpily. It didn't return the handshake.

So why did she decide to follow this mysterious cat? Nanami couldn't explain it.

All she knew was that from the moment she heard the cat's voice, she'd felt no fear. Far from it—she'd felt something closer to nostalgia.

Nanami knew what real fear felt like. On more than one occasion she'd thought she might die; unable to breathe properly, her head pounding, no longer able to hear the voices of people around her. And each time she'd hit this wall she had almost given up. Right now, on this most bizarre day, she wasn't going to give up on anything. Especially not on the day she'd met a talking cat.

"Wow! All these books . . ."

Following the cat down the passageway, she looked around and sighed contentedly. First, they'd passed by the usual French Literature shelves but then Nanami found herself walking down an unfamiliar passageway lined with bookshelves bathed in a soft, bluish light. The shelves on both sides were filled with books that she had never seen before. It wasn't only the titles that were new to her; they had bindings and lettering with symbols she didn't recognize. Some were bound in leather or cloth, while others were wrapped in no more than a couple of sheets of faded paper. These shelves extended into the distance, stuffed from top to bottom with an incredible variety of reading material.

"And yet there are fewer books in the world than ever," the cat remarked.

"Fewer books? What do you mean?"

"The human mind is getting weaker, I suppose. Pity."

The cat didn't sound particularly bothered.

"Anyway, that's not what we should be concerned about right now."

"Yes, the books that have been taken," said Nanami. "The man who stole them is down here?"

"That's right. But he's always on the move. We may not actually run into him."

"If we do see him, what's the plan?"

"Talk to him."

Surprised at the rational reply, Nanami stared at the cat. Undeterred, it explained further.

"I told you already, in this labyrinth the strongest thing is the power of truth. Lies are completely useless. Therefore, to get those books back you will have to speak the truth that comes from within you."

"How do you have a discussion with the kind of person who just takes books because he feels like it?"

The cat suddenly went quiet. The tapping of Nanami's shoes was the only sound.

"That's a very astute observation," it said finally.

"Your answers are making me nervous."

"You're right to feel nervous. There are plenty of human beings who have already been taken in by his words and, as a result, been unable to get their books back."

Nanami was silenced by these ominous words.

"Don't worry," the cat went on, "it's not as if you're going to die. You'll just lose all the memories that you associated with those books. Oh, and then you'll never have the chance to read them again."

"That would be a serious problem."

"Well, what do you know? That's the first time we've agreed on something. It'd be a problem for me too."

Nanami grimaced at the bitterness in the cat's tone.

"But I believe I can handle this," she said.

"That's surprising. What makes you think that?"

"I don't know," replied Nanami with utter calm. "I just have a feeling that everything will be okay."

Nanami didn't really get it herself. Walking with this cat, all her anxiety and nerves seemed to melt away. The cat turned and threw her a cold glance.

"Baseless optimism is a dangerous thing. 'And you all know, security is mortals' chiefest enemy.'"

Nanami was a little taken aback.

"Wow. I never thought I would hear a quote from *Hamlet* in a situation like this."

"Then again, I suppose rather than whining and complaining the whole time, a little optimism wouldn't hurt," continued the cat. "Especially as the future is uncertain."

"You really are perverse, aren't you?"

"Obviously. That's how cats are."

Tiger's voice echoed around the passageway rather more strongly than necessary.

As they walked, the air grew gradually brighter.

"By the way," said the cat, more softly this time, "it's not *Hamlet*. It's *Macbeth*."

Its voice was swallowed up by a brilliant white light.

As the bright light began to fade Nanami was astonished by what she saw. The stacks of books that had lined the passageway were nowhere to be seen. Instead, she and the cat were standing on a dirt road with ruts running along it, and the bookshelves on either side had become lines of evergreen trees. Bright sun shone from the sky and Nanami put her hand to her forehead to shade her eyes.

"A castle . . . ?"

Indeed, at the end of the road stood a stone structure that could only be described as a castle. At the front were imposing ramparts and, beyond, castle walls and a large tower. Positioned at various spots along the walls were what resembled heraldic flags, except that they had no coat of arms; they were just solid gray. Soldiers stood guard, long-barreled guns that looked like old-fashioned muskets slung over their shoulders. The castle gateway was a giant arch from which a sturdy drawbridge suspended by a chain protruded across a deep moat.

It was most definitely a castle.

Suddenly the earth seemed to tremble as a horse-drawn carriage emerged from the woods behind the pair. Nanami jumped aside to let it pass and stared after it as it sped its way across the drawbridge and through the castle gate.

"There are so many soldiers," said Nanami as she observed the gate through which the carriage had disappeared. Guards with muskets were stationed on either side of that too.

"Are they going to shoot at us?" she asked.

"What's the matter? Did you suddenly get scared after all?"

"Personally, I think it's weirder if someone doesn't get scared when they see a gun," she retorted.

"Don't worry about them," said the cat with its customary nonchalance. "It's all for show. The truly powerful have no need to flaunt weapons. The weaker you are, the more you feel the need to show off."

With that it sauntered off toward the castle gate. Nanami scrambled along behind.

Eventually, they reached it, and the two guards standing on either side of the wooden bridge merely saluted them. Their guns remained still, but Nanami was startled when she saw the soldiers' faces. Both had pale, ashen complexions. Their expressions were blank, and their features were oddly nondescript; the moment she turned her eyes away, she couldn't recall what their faces had looked like.

"They have the exact same face, and they don't look at all well . . ." she said.

"Those are the gray men," replied the cat. "They're all the same."

Indeed, the soldiers visible beyond the gate, those standing guard high on the battlements, the ones taking care of the horses, and even the coachman who had just arrived, all had the same gray face. The contrast between the identical wan shade of their complexions and the bright sunshine that shone down on them was eerie.

"The gray men . . ." Nanami mused to herself as they went through the stone ramparts into the castle. I've read about them in a book."

"That's valuable information."

"What do you mean?"

"These days, not many people know about them anymore," said the cat, without looking back. "And yet, they are extremely dangerous. There used to be people who were aware of the threat, and they used to write about it in books. Now, most of that knowledge has been forgotten."

There was a trace of melancholy in the cat's otherwise detached tone.

"You say they've been forgotten, but I'm not sure I'll ever be able to get these creepy faces out of my head," Nanami commented.

"Cherish that sense of unease you're feeling. The entire world is gradually being engulfed in that grayness. Most people don't even notice how these beings have managed to blend themselves into everyday life."

Suddenly, it felt as if the sky had widened above their heads. It was because the stone walls on either side had come to an end, and they had emerged into a large open courtyard.

The scene there was even more bizarre.

Right in the center of the courtyard was what looked like an altar. On it a fire burned and black smoke billowed into the sky. The gray-faced soldiers were busy either carrying wooden crates over to the altar or taking objects out of those crates and hurling them onto the fire. Other soldiers stood erect and motionless, apparently standing guard over the area. Occasionally there were shouts and calls, but because everyone had the same pale, unchanging expression, the liveliness was only an illusion. The whole scene was oddly surreal.

There was a commotion right behind them. The horse-drawn wagon was back. It passed by Nanami and stopped in front of the altar. Soldiers immediately swarmed around it and began to use rakes and shovels to drag the cargo off the back of the wagon. Nanami frowned when she recognized the contents that tumbled to the ground.

They were books.

Books of all shapes and sizes were being scattered on the ground like trash.

"Those are all books?" she asked the cat.

"Yes. They're bringing in books from all over the world and burning them here."

"Why?"

"Because they think it's the right thing to do."

But that wasn't a reason.

The soldiers raked up the books from the ground and dumped them into the wooden crates. They then carried the crates over to the altar where they tossed the books one after another onto the fire. The flames leapt higher.

Watching the wagon leave again, Nanami turned to the cat.

"I'm afraid to ask. Are the Lupin books already in that fire?"

"I don't think so," replied the cat. "Only weak books get burned here. The gray men can't handle powerful books. Those get taken to another location. The question is where . . . ?"

As soon as the cat finished speaking, Nanami had the odd feeling someone was calling to her; she turned her head.

In fact, she hadn't heard a voice, but as she scanned her surroundings, her eye was drawn to a large tower on the other side of the courtyard. At the base of the tower was an impressive staircase, wide enough that five or six people could comfortably walk side by side.

"What's over there?" she asked.

"Well, clearly that's the main castle building—the donjon."

"I think they're in there."

Nanami had already set off walking. The cat narrowed its jade-green eyes a moment, then followed without another word.

Dodging around the smoking altar, Nanami approached the foot of the staircase. She came face-to-face with more of the identical gray-faced guards, but they barely reacted. They simply saluted her and made no move to block her way.

"Odd, isn't it?" the cat remarked. "I'm supposed to be your guide, but it seems as if you're the one guiding me."

Nanami smiled at the cat's comment, then began to climb.

The staircase wasn't particularly steep, although it had a lot of steps. When she finally reached the top, Nanami had to stop and put her hand to her chest. She took a deep breath.

"Are you okay?" the cat asked her.

"For now."

Honestly, Nanami was a bit worried about how her body would react. After all, she was here in this strange place, and her anxiety level was rising. They had already walked a considerable distance to get to the castle and now she'd climbed a long flight of stairs. There was no telling when some sudden movement might awaken the rampaging horse deep in her chest. Yet, strangely enough, right now she felt no fear, and her breathing remained calm.

"You're strong," remarked the cat.

"Not really. My friend Itsuka's always telling me I'm weak, so I should be careful."

"I'm not talking about physically. Mentally."

And with that cryptic comment, the cat turned its attention to the interior of the castle donjon. From the outside it had looked like a simple tower structure, but on the inside they found themselves at the start of a surprisingly long corridor. The ceiling was high, and a bright-red carpet led into the distance. Each side was lined with a row of thick columns, and in the smaller corridors that branched off here and there, they could see spiral staircases leading upward. A gray-faced soldier stood guard at the foot of each column.

Nanami now began to move forward along the corridor. Thanks to the thick carpet her footsteps made almost no sound at all. As she passed identical columns guarded by identical soldiers, she felt as if she had accidentally wandered into a world of optical illusion that she had once seen in a picture book.

Eventually Nanami and the cat found themselves in front of heavy wooden doors.

"Who goes there?" demanded the pallid-faced soldier guarding the door. His posture and his expression didn't change one iota, and his voice was entirely without inflection. He didn't even meet their eyes.

"Beyond this door is the General's Grand Hall. What is your business here?"

"We have come to speak to the General," replied the cat in a confident voice.

The soldier did not immediately respond. He turned his gray head slightly toward the cat and Nanami, his eyes expressionless.

Nanami winced, but after a few seconds the soldier abruptly straightened up and clicked his heels.

"Visitors for the General!" he shouted and, following a moment's pause, the phrase began to ring throughout the castle, as every soldier repeated the words in turn.

"Visitors for the General!"

"Visitors for the General!"

The exact same words, in the exact same voice and with the exact same intonation, echoed from the walls. Once the distant voices could no longer be heard, the great doors began slowly to swing open.

"Let's go."

The cat's calm low voice resonated through the space.

Beyond the doors the red carpet continued to run through a large room—a vast hall.

Opulent chandeliers hung from the ceiling. Beyond them at the far end of the hall the wall was draped with a plain gray hanging. Beneath that hanging, elevated three steps above the rest of the room on a kind of platform, was a crimson velvet armchair, placed in such a way as to exude an air of authority.

While the central carpet was brightly lit, the walls on either side were in the shadows. Nanami noticed soldiers standing rigidly to attention, several feet apart; she shuddered instinctively.

"This room doesn't feel very welcoming," she muttered.

"Don't be afraid. As I told you, those with true power do not flaunt their weapons needlessly," the cat reassured her, before setting off into the room.

As she followed, Nanami's gaze fell on a series of large white cubes placed at equal intervals along both sides of the carpet. From a distance, she'd been unable to make out what they were, but now she could see they were polished marble tables. They were about the size of the desks she often used at the library, though they had no drawers or even legs; they were simply pure white cubes. It was as if someone had lined up rows of giant white dice.

Her eye was caught by what was displayed on the top of one of these dice.

"It's *Twenty Thousand Leagues Under the Sea*," she said in amazement.

Unmistakably, Jules Verne's masterpiece lay open on the table.

"And this is one of the volumes of *The Lord of the Rings*. It's been displayed here like some sort of national treasure."

In fact, on each of the marble tables—there were between ten and twenty of them—was a different work of literature, illuminated by the bright chandeliers overhead.

"*Doctor Dolittle . . . Treasure Island . . . Moby-Dick . . .*"

"Are you familiar with all these?" asked the cat.

"They're the books that I had the best time reading. They're all like friends to me."

"I see. You are truly blessed with friends."

Nanami went from table to table, discovering on one *The Three Musketeers*, and other volumes from the D'Artagnan series, and on another the children's picture book *Frederick*. They were all books that had previously vanished from the library. When she arrived at the table nearest to the velvet armchair, she stopped.

Sitting on the polished white marble were ten well-worn books. Their spines were faded, and their corners tattered in a way that Nanami recognized. Here were the missing volumes of *Arsène Lupin, Gentleman Thief*.

"Well, you are very unexpected guests."

With a start, Nanami looked up. On the platform above her stood a large man dressed in a gray suit and matching deerstalker hat. It was the man from the library. He was flanked by two guards, each sporting an array of shiny medals.

A bright red carpet, a vast hall, soldiers in old-fashioned uniforms—in the midst of this scene stood the man in the suit, perfectly calm and composed. That in itself was bizarre enough, but as the man removed his deerstalker cap, Nanami shrank back, repulsed.

He had the same gray expressionless face as all the soldiers. However, unlike the soldiers' vacant, puppetlike appearance, this man had distinctive features. A prominent hooked nose, a jet-black mustache, and piercing gray eyes gave him a striking presence.

The man deposited his cap into the hands of one of the guards, ran his eyes over Nanami appraisingly, and gave a perfunctory bow.

"Welcome to the General's Grand Hall."

"The General's Grand Hall?"

"Yes, the grand hall that belongs to the General," the man repeated with a grandiose air.

"And you're the General?"

"Needless to say."

With a grand flourish, the Gray General offered his right hand.

"I am so glad you came. We hardly ever get visitors here. You are most welcome."

Just as in a concert hall, the huge room reverberated with the General's deep voice. Outwardly at least, he seemed calm and courteous, but along with it he projected an intense feeling of threat.

His gaze shifted downward to the vicinity of Nanami's feet and his thick eyebrows furrowed.

"So you're here too," he said. "It's been a while. I thought you might have given up by now."

Nanami glanced down at her companion.

"Do you know each other?" she asked.

"I'm afraid we do," the cat replied coldly. "But we're not friends."

Tiger glared at the man on the platform.

"General, we've come to take back the books."

"I'm so sick of hearing that same tired old line," said the General. "I've already told you, it's for the sake of humanity. Are you determined to stand in the way of that?"

"Well, that's one heck of an excuse," muttered Nanami. "You took these books without permission and now you claim it was for the good of humanity? Mr. Hamura would be outraged if he heard that."

"You're a brave girl."

The General had picked up immediately on Nanami's mumbled protest.

"You misunderstand me," he went on. "It's true that we are the ones taking the books from the library; it's an inevitability, it's a necessity, it's unavoidable, and it must be done."

"I'm not sure about you, but when I want to take a book from the library, I have to observe the proper borrowing procedure. It doesn't matter whether you're a junior high school pupil or a general, it's against the rules to take a book without going via the checkout counter."

It was true. Nanami couldn't help wishing that Old Ham had been there right now to explain the procedure with a good helping of sarcasm and snide remarks.

The General continued to smile, and he even raised an eyebrow in apparent admiration.

"Not only brave, but such a wise young girl."

He turned around and arranged himself in the armchair behind him, a gray-faced man in a gray suit in an opulent velvet chair. He crossed his legs. On either side of him stood the guards with their old-fashioned muskets. The scene was lit by the bright light of the chandeliers overhead.

Something was wrong. The whole scene was odd, mismatched somehow. It was like a badly composed photograph.

"I don't think you've grasped the situation yet," continued the General. "Therefore, I recommend that you avoid jumping to conclusions. We are acting on your behalf. You will understand in time."

The gray-suited General gazed up at the glittering chandelier with melancholy eyes.

"It's very difficult to burn a book." He sighed. "I think you saw that on your way here. The courtyard below is filled with books from all over the world, and the soldiers have to work extremely hard to keep them burning. The books just keep on arriving and it's a full-time task to keep reducing them to ash and smoke. And even then, not all the books submit to being incinerated. The more powerful books put up quite a fight."

The General raised a hand to indicate the hall before him.

"Once all those powerful books are gathered here in this room, we must wait for their power to weaken. Here they lie in state, and once they've faded from people's memory, even the most resilient of books will find it difficult to resist forever. That is what this hall is for."

"May I ask you a very basic question?" said Nanami matter-of-factly, her voice also echoing through the space.

The General lowered his right hand and extended it in Nanami's direction.

"Go ahead."

"Why are you burning books?"

"Well, that's simple," he replied, stroking his mustache. "Because they're dangerous."

Nanami was completely taken aback by this unexpected answer. The General got to his feet and began to pace the platform as if it were his stage, and he some great actor.

"Books are extremely dangerous," he announced, "especially the old ones that have been passed down from generation to generation—the ones that countless people throughout time and throughout the world have held in their hands."

"Books are dangerous?"

"Yes, dangerous. Well, of course, I am not saying that all books are dangerous. There are plenty of harmless books that contain common knowledge. And I don't deny the usefulness of the kind that provide people with simple entertainment. But the majority of books aren't like that. Particularly the ones you see lined up here. They lead people astray."

Of course, Nanami's silence wasn't because she was convinced by the General's words. It was because her personal attachment to books was at least double or perhaps even three times greater than the average person's. If there had been an obvious counterargument, she would have launched into it immediately. But this man's speech was so ridiculous that she couldn't see a way to respond. None of it made the slightest bit of sense.

"The world is changing at a tremendous pace."

The General strode to the left end of the platform, then turned with a flourish, and set off back again.

"There is nothing useful to be gained from old books. In fact, they are full of mistakes. And yet, there are people who insist on reading them and clinging to the worthless trash that was written in former times. Just look at what we've got lined up here. Every one of them outdated, stuck in the ugly and perverse traditions of the past. People mustn't be constrained by the ways of bygone days. Human beings are freer now. They lead far richer lives than ever before."

"That doesn't mean—"

It wasn't that Nanami had finally found the words to fight back, but she'd realized if she didn't jump in soon the General's speech might go on for eternity.

"That doesn't mean that you need to burn these books. To read them, or not to read them, that's all you have to decide. It's up to the individual."

"That's delusional."

The General gave her a pitying look.

"Take this musket, for example."

He approached one of the guards and reached out to stroke the polished barrel of the gun the man was holding, almost as if petting a small animal.

"A musket, at first glance, is a seemingly harmless and elegant decorative object. But in someone's hands, it becomes an extremely dangerous piece of equipment. With no more than the movement of a forefinger, you can shoot and kill the person standing in front of you. The same goes for books. No problem with a bunch of old books if they're just there to make your bookshelf look good. But plenty of people handle them carelessly. Thus, we are doing all we can to gather up those books as quickly as possible and turn them into ashes."

The General removed his hand from the gun barrel and turned back to Nanami. He was perfectly composed.

"It's all right. You don't have to worry your head with anything too complex."

His arrogant posture and tone remained the same; now, though, there was a touch of sweetness in his voice. Nanami felt her body begin to relax and for a moment had a strange sensation as if she was being gently lifted off her feet and hugged by the soothing sound.

"There's no need to fret. Just leave everything to us."

That deep persuasive voice filled the entire hall, enveloping everything in the space. The General opened his arms as if to embrace not only Nanami's misgivings, but her whole being.

For a second she stood entranced. Then she shook her head as if to rid herself of the suffocating warmth that clung to her, and glared back at her opponent. What she saw made her gasp. His eyes were as blank as two glass beads.

Something was definitely wrong . . .

And then came another thought—one that almost escaped into that vast empty space; just in time she reached out and grasped hold of it, hauling it back into her mind.

Those words of the General, *There's no need to worry. Just leave everything to us*. They were words that should normally have been reassuring to the listener, offering peace of mind. But right here, right now, they felt distorted.

She put her hand to her neck. Although it wasn't hot in the room, she was sweating. A very unpleasant cold sweat.

"You see how terrifying this man is?" said the cat. Its tone was grave, but its low voice had a calming effect on Nanami.

"Yes, it's all wrong. He is so imposing, and full of confidence, and yet . . . There's something very creepy about him."

"You must have a strong heart to be able to sense that. As I told you before—truth and the power of the heart are everything here."

"But the truth—"

"This General has a twisted way of fighting. He doesn't reveal the truth of his intentions. He appears to speak, but in fact he says nothing. He sucks the truth from his visitors and turns it into his own power."

Difficult words to comprehend.

The cat continued in its down-to-earth way.

"Not everyone has a heart as strong as yours. In fact, most people don't. These weak-hearted people easily fall prey to other people's overconfidence. Making your own decisions and acting for yourself requires taking responsibility. And so, these people stop thinking for themselves. It's easier to leave everything up to somebody else. And that's how eventually they end up abandoning their own personal truths."

"Is that what you meant when you said 'plenty of human beings have already been taken in by his words'?"

"That's right. It doesn't even matter what the General says in his speeches. Those who have abandoned their own truths just stop thinking altogether. They sink into a childlike delusion that some great general oozing with confidence will solve everything for them. There's nothing more comfortable than dozing off without a care in the world in the back seat of a car being driven by your father. They don't even consider that there will come a time when they'll have to take the wheel themselves. Many adults, no matter how old they get, remain children at heart."

Nanami felt as if she was suffocating, although this time it wasn't from her asthma. Honestly, she wasn't sure about the strength of her heart, but she knew that no one would protect her fragile body besides herself. If she were ever to stop thinking for herself, it would be like lying down and waiting for some kind person to notice her asthma attack. And that was a very scary scenario indeed.

"Well, girl?"

The General's booming voice interrupted her thoughts. She looked up at him standing proudly on his platform, arms outstretched as before.

"It's decision time," he announced. "Come along . . . Well, actually there's no need for you to decide anything. You can follow me with perfect peace of mind."

His two hollow beads were fixed on Nanami. A strong voice, commanding gestures, gentle words, and a subtle smile . . .

Behind these was absolutely nothing.

"Who are you?"

She hadn't thought about it; the question just spilled out. Her voice may have been small, but it still echoed around the General's Grand Hall.

The General raised an eyebrow.

"Well, I didn't expect that. You're the first visitor who has ever asked me that question."

"There's something very odd about you."

The General didn't react.

"Something seems off to me. For sure."

"What kind of thing?"

"I don't know exactly, but it feels as if something important is missing."

The General seemed surprised by this. He cocked his head slightly and stroked his mustache with two fat fingers.

"I see. That may well be true," he muttered. "No, you're probably right."

He turned his chilling gaze back on Nanami.

"Very well. Out of respect, I'm going to give you a clue. I'm the one who walks beside you."

The voice that echoed in the shadows was controlled but completely devoid of feeling. Oppressive and heavy, and at the same time as shapeless as water.

He stopped next to his armchair and made a show of pulling a pocket watch from his breast pocket.

"I'm terribly sorry, it's time. I have to go and collect the next books. There are still so many harmful books out there in the world."

He took his deerstalker cap from the guard and turned back to Nanami.

"There's no more to say. Go home. Of course, you'll need to say goodbye to all the books in this room. Take those good old stories and stash them in the storeroom of your mind. And while you're at it, make sure you lock them away properly. That way they won't lead you back here again."

Hat in hand, he bowed deeply. It was a sign that this meeting was over.

Nanami remained motionless as the General, flanked by his two guards, stepped down from the platform.

"Nanami?"

Ignoring the cat, she turned and walked over to the closest marble table.

"I may not understand all the complex stuff," she said, "but I do know one thing for sure."

She reached out a small hand toward the book in front of her.

"I never forget a precious book."

Right as the tips of her fingers were about to touch the book's cover, there was an earsplitting explosion. After the reverberations died down, Nanami heard the voice of the General.

"You can't do that. That's part of my collection."

She looked up to see that the General had stopped at the edge of the platform. On either side of him the guards had their muskets aimed straight at Nanami. Not only that, every soldier along the walls of the hall was pointing a gun either at the girl or at the cat.

Nanami tried to meet his gaze, but hesitated. She saw something sinister beneath the cold, glassy stare.

"Don't worry, that was just a blank," the General said.

"But, as I mentioned earlier, these muskets can be dangerous weapons. I can't speak for the next shot."

Nanami was aware that sweat was pouring from her. She looked down at the cat by her feet.

"I thought you said that this was all for show," she muttered.

"I stand corrected. He has definitely become more powerful. He's not like he used to be."

"How did he used to be?"

Rather than reply, the cat began slowly to back away.

"We'll have to go, Nanami. It's not a good idea to anger the General."

"You mean run away?"

The cat seemed taken aback by the strength of this reaction.

Nanami had no intention of backing down. She stayed exactly where she was, looking at the General on his platform. She paid no heed to any of the soldiers or the guns they were pointing at her. Of course, she wasn't completely without fear, but there was another, fierce emotion bubbling up in her chest. The General had said that the books were dangerous, and that was why he was burning them. She didn't know what that meant, and if she fled now without ever fully understanding, then she would regret it forever. She was sure, and had been from the moment she had stepped into that pale blue glowing aisle of bookcases, that today was not a day to give up.

And that was the moment it happened . . .

All at once she was surrounded by a pale light. She turned

in surprise to see that several of the books lined up on the marble tables had begun to glow. As she watched, their soft light became brighter and brighter until the whole of the General's Grand Hall was filled with a dazzling radiance.

"What's happening?"

For the first time, a look of confusion appeared on the General's face. In the same moment, the soldiers who had been aiming their muskets at Nanami and the cat began to panic, dashing around in a bizarrely frantic manner. All their earlier mechanical precision had vanished. Some of them even tried to flee and ended up colliding with other soldiers around them.

Twenty Thousand Leagues Under the Sea sparkled.

Beneath the Wheel was shimmering.

Frederick and *The Very Hungry Caterpillar* both began to radiate a dazzling whiteness.

"Don't panic!" shouted the General at his soldiers. "It's just the books fussing."

The soldiers weren't listening. They were so terrified it was almost comical. Some of them lay down on the floor with their hands over their heads.

On the other hand, although the glare of the books was intense, Nanami didn't feel the slightest discomfort, let alone danger. A wonderfully warm, invigorating feeling was growing in her chest.

"Hey," she said in a whisper, "how far can a cat run?"

"What are you talking about?" said the cat. But then, grasping Nanami's intention, its eyes grew wide.

Around them, books were radiating light, and the soldiers

were in disarray. Some clung to pillars or stood trembling, their eyes tightly shut.

"It's too risky. I've no idea how powerful those muskets are."

"So we're just going to flee home with our tails between our legs?" Nanami asked.

"I hate to admit it, but I see no other choice."

Then the cat realized something.

"What about you? How far can you run? Are you even able to?"

"For about a minute," Nanami replied. "If you let me do some warm-up exercises, I think I can go for a little longer."

Nanami was doing her best to add a little humor to the situation, but the cat wasn't amused. It looked as if the books weren't going to stay lit up indefinitely; already some of their lights were growing dimmer. If they stopped shining completely, there was a risk that the soldiers' panic might subside.

"We can't take them all. I'm going to grab one book and take it back with me."

"This kid . . ." muttered the cat. Nanami threw him a sharp look.

"I already told you. I never forget a precious book."

There was a faint smile on her lips.

The cat was speechless for a moment, then it exhaled deeply.

"Right then. I'm counting on you."

That was the signal.

In a flash, Nanami had grabbed *The Hollow Needle* from the Arsène Lupin collection and dashed for the exit.

It seemed the General hadn't expected the move, as all he

could do was roar incomprehensibly. He set off after Nanami and his voice changed to a scream.

"Stop!"

As Nanami fled, the light throughout the room seemed to shine even more brilliantly, as if to aid her escape. She passed through the door and was out of the General's Grand Hall, only to discover that the rest of the soldiers throughout the castle must have heard the commotion and had begun to assemble on the steps at the entrance to the donjon. The light from the General's Grand Hall didn't have the power to reach that far.

The cat swiftly changed direction and dashed into a side corridor, Nanami right behind. In the shadow of one of the massive columns they spotted a spiral staircase. Still following the cat's lead, Nanami ran up the staircase in a single breath, emerging at the top of the castle wall. By some stroke of luck, all the soldiers who'd been stationed there had already run down and gathered below, leaving no one up there under the line of gray flags fluttering in the wind. Nanami and the cat ran headlong along the deserted battlements, the wind whistling around them.

"It's been years since I ran like this . . ."

Nanami's thoughts were interrupted by a sudden burst of sound. The soldiers around the altar in the courtyard were firing up at the battlements. As the shots rang out, Nanami clutched the book even tighter to her chest.

"Can those all be blanks?"

"Don't think about it!"

There was a small tower at the end of the wall, directly above the castle gate. Going down the steps inside that tower would be the fastest way out of the castle.

When they reached it, Nanami felt a strange sensation in her throat.

"I don't think I can last much longer."

"Just a little more. What's happened to that spirit of yours?"

"Don't push it. I'm doing the best I can," replied Nanami.

As they started to hurry down the stairs, they realized that soldiers were coming up the staircase from below. The sound of their marching feet, steady and rhythmic, grew louder with each step. The pair turned and ran back up, only to find a column of soldiers marching toward them along the same path they'd just taken. The soldiers all wore that same gray face and identical blank expression. It was a haunting sight.

"Mission failed . . ." Nanami muttered. She gave a wry smile, her breath coming in faint wheezes. Bayonets drawn, the soldiers approached in an almost laughably perfect formation.

"What's going to happen now?" she asked the cat.

"I don't know."

"I'll never be able to go home, will I?"

"I don't know that, either."

The cat shook its head and turned its jade-green eyes toward the approaching soldiers.

"I owe you an apology," it said. "I should never have brought you here. I was too naive."

Doing her best to control her breathing, Nanami knelt down and laid a hand softly on the cat's head.

"At times like this, there's no apology necessary. In fact, I want to thank you. After all, we came here together."

The cat, rather confused, watched Nanami wipe the sweat from her forehead and smile.

"Actually, I had a lot of fun."

And that was when a tiny door in the top of the tower swung open. It was right behind them, but until now, neither of them had noticed it. At the same time, they heard a voice.

"This way!"

Nanami looked at the cat.

"A friend of yours?"

"I've no idea."

"Not very helpful," muttered Nanami.

And with that hasty exchange, the girl and the cat threw themselves at the door. The moment they passed through, it shut behind them. In that instant all the chaos of the General's Grand Hall and battlements—the yelling and gunfire—vanished as if it had never existed.

Pressing her hand to her chest, Nanami looked around her. She'd expected to find herself on the stone floor of a tiny castle room, but this was way beyond her expectations. Before her was a long passageway, bathed once more in a bluish-white light, lined on either side with endless rows of bookcases, packed with row and rows of books.

It was the same mysterious passageway they'd taken to get here.

"Looks like you made it just in time."

The voice was gentle. Its owner stepped away from the door

he had just closed and moved into the light. It was a young bespectacled man with a friendly smile on his face. Even though he wasn't particularly tall, the way he moved with ease gave him a larger presence. He looked to be in his mid-twenties. He observed Nanami with calm, intelligent eyes.

"Nanami?" the cat called to her. "Before anything, take your medication."

Nanami was jolted back to reality. Still sitting on the floor, she took her inhaler from her pocket and put it to her mouth. She began to breathe in but was overtaken by a fit of coughing. Her vision became blurry.

The young man knelt down beside her.

"With a bit of a rest do you think you'll be able to walk?" he said, rubbing her back.

"Maybe . . . I think so."

"Don't push yourself," he said, "but if you think you can manage it, we'd better start moving. Get away from this place."

Despite the urgency of the situation, the man seemed relaxed, and there was no sense of haste or pressure on her. After listening to the General's oppressive voice, this young man's way of speaking soothed Nanami's heart and filled her with a pleasant warmth.

The man reached for the copy of *The Hollow Needle* that Nanami had placed by her feet.

"You did well to bring this back with you."

"Do you know that book?"

"Of course. It's one of the most famous books ever written."

There was a hint of humor in his words.

The man returned the book to Nanami, then turned to address the cat.

"It's been a while."

The jade eyes flashed at him, but for a while there was no response. After a few moments, the cat opened its mouth and spoke in its usual detached tone.

"Yes. How many years has it been now?"

"Must be ten or so."

"That long! . . . No wonder you've gotten taller."

As Nanami looked on in wonder, the young man grinned and nodded. A hint of a smile even seemed to cross the unsociable feline's features.

She couldn't help but interrupt.

"Do you two know each other?"

"Yes, we're old friends," said the cat.

And all of sudden it smiled fondly at the young man.

"Thank you for coming, Mr. Proprietor," it said.

The man nodded again, this time with great warmth.

THE ONE WHO WAS CREATED

"You okay, Nanami?"

Itsuka climbed to the top of the long flight of stairs at the train station and turned her head to check on her friend. Nanami, right behind her, took a breath before answering.

"Don't worry. I'm taking it slowly."

She put a hand gingerly to her chest. So far, so good—no dangerous signs. She took a deep breath and started back up the steps.

It was a Sunday morning; there weren't many people about. Still, the stairs of this unfamiliar train station seemed to go on for much longer than she'd expected. It had been unusually cold when she'd gotten up that morning, so she'd wrapped up warm; now she felt beads of sweat on her forehead. She was unaccustomed to getting this much exercise, and she was also nervous. For now, her asthma was under control, but Nanami knew that if she got too carried away and broke into a run, then it wouldn't turn out well for her. She kept her pace slow and steady, one step at a time.

"I don't think I've ever traveled this far before."

Itsuka's response was direct as always. "That's because you only ever go from your house to the school and the library."

"Today might be the first time I've ever taken the train without my dad."

Itsuka looked surprised by this, but she knew better than to offer unnecessary words of sympathy.

"Once I had an asthma attack on the train and had to be taken by ambulance from the station, so I don't think he wants me to travel without him."

"But he was okay with you going this time?"

"I didn't mention anything about taking the train. I just said I was going to hang out with Itsuka."

"Whoa, Nanami!"

Itsuka looked shocked.

"Well, if I'd asked, he'd never have let me come," said Nanami with a nervous laugh.

Right then a group of four or five elementary school boys came tearing at full speed up the stairs and passed by Nanami like a gust of wind.

"The other day I was a little late getting home, and he was so mad at me," she continued.

"I guess he worries about you."

"That's part of it, although I also think he's exhausted from work recently. He comes home late so often. I think he should pay more attention to his own health."

Nanami's father used to take her to the library all the time; it was a distant memory now.

"It's the same for me. Both my parents work nonstop from morning to night. Always so busy that they barely spend any time with us. Dual income, but somehow we're still struggling with money. It's a tough old world, isn't it?"

Nanami couldn't help smiling at her friend's oddly adult turn of phrase.

They finally reached the top of the stairs, and Itsuka turned to look at her.

"Will you be okay on your own from here?"

"I'll be fine. You've got to get to your archery tournament. I really appreciate that you came this far with me."

"It's not a major tournament—just a regional meet. I promise you if I didn't have to go, I'd have stuck with you to the end."

"No problem. You've been a great help."

"Let me just check one more time," Itsuka said, adjusting her grip on her bow. "You say you absolutely have to go to this 'Natsuki Books'?"

Nanami nodded.

"I'm not even sure what I'm doing. I simply know that I have to go and figure out what's going on."

Nanami knew that this was a vague answer at best, but there was nothing else to say. It was only a week since the mysterious events of the library.

———

On the day in question, Nanami had returned through the passageway of soft bluish-white light, not back to the library where her journey had begun but to a totally unfamiliar location.

Just like the library, the passageway was lined with bookcases on both sides, although their appearance was completely different. When she emerged, the bookshelves around her weren't made of basic steel; instead they were of well-worn wood, polished until it gleamed. Old-fashioned lamps hung from the ceiling, and in the middle of the single long aisle stood a desk with an elegant porcelain tea set.

"This is Natsuki Books," said the young man who had led her there. "And I'm Rintaro Natsuki."

Nanami couldn't forget the gently shining eyes behind the man's glasses as he introduced himself. The rest of her memories, however, were all hazy, probably because she had still been suffering an asthma attack. She'd been gasping for breath as Rintaro had led her to a chair, covered her with a blanket, and prepared her a pot of tea.

By the time she'd finished her cup of hot black tea with milk, and her breathing had calmed down, the cat had vanished, and the passageway of light had faded away to be replaced by an unremarkable wooden wall.

"I was just closing up the shop when suddenly the back wall began to glow," Rintaro had explained to a still-dazed Nanami. "It's been a very long time since I've seen it do that, so it took me totally by surprise. But I realized at once that I was needed, so I leapt into the light. And there you both were."

Rintaro recounted all this as if it was completely normal. He made no attempt to elaborate on what he meant by *it's been a very long time*, but Rintaro was hesitant.

"It's not easy to explain. It's like being asked to give a brief summary of a book that I love."

"Now, that I can understand," Nanami had said emphatically, her hands wrapped around the warm teacup. "I wouldn't know where to start if you asked me to express all the emotions stirred up by *The Three Musketeers*."

Rintaro smiled with delight at her response.

The little clock on the desk showed it was after 7:00 p.m.

Considering all that had happened, a relatively short amount of time had passed. Still, it wasn't the time of the evening for a second-year junior high school girl to be out. What's more, Rintaro's bookshop was quite a ways from the town where Nanami lived. Rintaro had ended up driving her home.

The whole episode had been like a dream. So many things

had happened that Nanami was left feeling dizzy. But the worst part had come after that.

At home, her father was waiting for her stern-faced. Nanami's faint hope that he might not be back from work yet was instantly dashed.

"Where've you been till this time?"

The harsh tone was to be expected. For a girl who went nowhere except school, the library, and her own home, it was the first time she had ever been out beyond nightfall. Obviously she couldn't tell her father about the cat and the castle with the gray men. She managed to assuage her father's anger by apologizing and saying she'd been at Itsuka's house.

After enduring about an hour of her father's lecturing, a rather misplaced sense of nostalgia crept in as it occurred to Nanami that this was the first time in ages that the two of them had spent so much time in each other's company. Recently her father hadn't been around at all, and the rare time that he came home early from work, she barely caught a glimpse of his exhausted face, let alone had the chance to have a proper conversation.

Finally, her father had finished his lecture, and Nanami went to her room looking chastened. But only half of her mind was feeling sorry; the other half had plenty of other things to occupy it.

"Come back and visit anytime"—Rintaro's parting words as he handed her a piece of paper with his address and a map to the shop.

A cat, a young man, and a mysterious bookshop.

Even though her father had told her off, not going back wasn't an option. She'd been amazed at her own boldness, and she'd decided to ask Itsuka's opinion too.

"You know the way to the bookshop?"

The sound of Itsuka's voice brought Nanami back from her daydream. She was holding the map that Rintaro had given her; this was her first time walking in an unfamiliar town. She looked around and spotted bus stops and a taxi stand; beyond them, a long row of shops. It was typical of any station area anywhere in Japan, but to Nanami it was a brand-new adventure.

Her eye on the passing traffic, Itsuka casually brought up a question.

"So, if I were to go to that bookshop, I'd meet a talking cat?"

Nanami gave her friend the side-eye.

"You don't believe me, do you?"

"Would anyone believe something like that?"

"Nah, I guess not," Nanami responded with a grimace. "Still, how come you've come all this way with me?"

Itsuka appeared to be thinking it over. When she finally replied, it was without the hint of a smile.

"I guess it's because we're friends."

It was only Itsuka who could say something like that.

Nanami would have liked to support Itsuka the way her

friend always supported her, but she was limited in what she could offer. At the very least, she was determined never to lie to her friend, and so she had shared with Itsuka everything she could about the mysterious happenings of a week earlier. Itsuka had listened in amazement, somehow managing neither to laugh nor interrupt the story until Nanami had finished telling it. Then she had said one single sentence:

"What can I do to help?"

Of course, Nanami already knew what she needed.

"Honestly, Nanami, when you asked me to go with you on this trip, I thought you needed to get your head examined," Itsuka said now.

"Hey!"

"I'm just kidding. Look, take care and try not to overdo it."

Itsuka hoisted up her bow wrapped in its black cloth and turned to leave. Nanami found herself calling after her.

"Itsuka?"

"Yes?" said Itsuka, turning to look back at her friend.

"I owe you a steamed meat bun next time."

Itsuka raised an eyebrow slightly at the offer, but there was still no difference in her demeanor.

"Got it," she said, and she was off down the station steps.

Nanami watched her go, then, slipping the map back into her pocket, she set out into the unfamiliar town.

She walked along the main shopping street, made two turns, and found herself in a quiet residential area. It was a little hilly, and the road climbed gently, lined by two-story houses with traditional tiled roofs. Cars were parked in the driveways, children's bicycles lined up alongside, and the sidewalk was punctuated with drink vending machines. Past all of this, Nanami strolled at her own pace as several children the age of the boys she'd seen earlier at the station dashed by, footballs under their arms. She guessed there was an elementary school nearby.

Eventually she stopped in front of a little two-story shop. Attached to the polished latticework door was a wooden nameplate: "Natsuki Books." She'd been there less than a week ago but had been too preoccupied to take in the exterior of the shop properly, let alone its surroundings.

Looking around now, Nanami saw plant pots lined up each side of the pleasantly sunlit doorway, scarlet poinsettias ruffled by the passing breeze. It was a simple shop front with no special adornments, looking more like an antique shop than a bookshop, but Nanami felt it perfectly matched the image of the mild-mannered young proprietor.

She opened the lattice door and peeked in and was greeted by the relaxed tones of someone who seemed to have been expecting her.

"Thank you for coming all this way, Nanami-chan."

Farther down the bookshop's long aisle, Rintaro was standing behind the desk with its cash register.

"Hello," said Nanami, nervously bowing her head. She took another look around.

The shop front was narrow but the interior was deep. The long narrow aisle was lined on both sides with heavy wooden shelves that reached up to the ceiling and were chock-full of books. Behind the desk in the middle, a staircase led up to the second floor, and it seemed Rintaro had just come down those stairs.

"Have you been okay since last week?"

Rintaro's voice was warm and full of concern. Nanami was quick to reply.

"I've been just fine. I'm so sorry that I worried you."

"Actually, I was more worried whether you'd make it here with that terrible scribbled map I gave you. As I expected, though, nothing would faze Nanami-chan."

"You know I'm already in junior high school. I'm not really comfortable with being called 'Nanami-chan,'" she retorted.

Rintaro had such a pleasant and laid-back air about him that Nanami felt comfortable being so direct. He smiled and nodded, then gestured to her to sit by him.

"Right, Nanami. First, shall we have a cup of tea?"

His manner was completely natural, as if welcoming a regular customer. In this place, strange encounters and mysterious happenings were somehow perfectly normal everyday events.

"I had a feeling you were going to pay me a visit soon," he remarked, as he poured freshly boiled water into the teapot.

"How did you know?" Nanami asked.

"Well, of course I couldn't be sure," he said with a shake of his head. "For some reason, I just got that feeling..."

He really was an enigmatic type, Nanami thought. It wasn't

easy to imagine him ever getting flustered or being surprised. She guessed she must be an odd sort of visitor for him. After all, the first time she'd turned up here, she hadn't entered through the door, but through a solid wall.

Although, speaking of strange happenings, Rintaro's sudden materialization to rescue her was also very curious. The current atmosphere wasn't right for delving into such mysteries now, though. It was purely welcoming.

As Rintaro set out the teacups with a practiced hand, Nanami turned her attention to the bookshop.

Tolstoy, Hesse, Kafka, Nietzsche, all those distinguished names arranged side by side, the full canon of their works. Dostoevsky was intimidating just by his presence, but the names of Kawabata Yasunari and Natsume Sōseki, written in familiar kanji characters, were somehow comforting. Even though there were books that Nanami had read, she felt as if she had barely crossed the threshold into the world of such profound literature.

The exquisite cloth binding of *The Iliad* and the gorgeous arabesque cover design of *The Canterbury Tales* made you want to snatch them up. The titles of Čapek's *R.U.R. (Rossum's Universal Robots)* and Mann's *The Magic Mountain* had long since caught her imagination, and she already planned to read them.

She could see that every book had been placed with the greatest of care. Last time she was here, she'd been in no state to really observe her surroundings; now her heart beat faster just being able to take it all in. For a while, Nanami gazed up at the shelves, utterly entranced.

"This is a really beautiful bookshop."

"That's a very interesting critique. I'm often told it's old, or unique, but that's the first time anyone's called it beautiful."

"I think it's truly beautiful."

"If there are any books you'd like, go ahead and take them."

As Rintaro tipped the pot to fill the two cups, the air filled with a fresh aroma with a hint of sweetness.

"This isn't a library, though, is it?"

"No problem. When you finish reading a book, you put it back, and it's the same as it was to start with. This is a used bookshop."

Nanami laughed at how unlike a regular bookshop owner he sounded.

"It feels as if you know everything about the world, Rintaro-san."

"Why do you say that?"

"Because all this weird stuff is happening, and you don't even question it. It's as if you understand it all already."

"That's not it. It's just that I'm a little older than you."

Rintaro purposely kept his explanation simple. He didn't want to rattle off a bunch of words and overwhelm Nanami.

Nanami understood that rushing into an explanation meant you might in fact get further away from the answer. The same way that racing too quickly up a long flight of steps meant she risked having an asthma attack and being unable to go on. Taking things steadily, one step at a time, meant she would eventually make it to the exit.

"Maybe I've been waiting for this a long time."

As Rintaro spoke, he placed a cup of tea in front of his guest. Then, taking his own cup in his hand, he leaned back against the nearest bookcase.

"Lately I've had the sense that something cold and empty has been spreading through the world," he went on. "I can't easily explain where that feeling came from, but I don't think it's just my imagination."

"Something cold and empty?"

"I can't really express it properly; that's the only way I can find to put it. That coldness is starting to creep into people's hearts and crush them."

"You're talking about those gray men?" Nanami asked at once.

The image of a gray-faced man in a gray suit floated into her mind. The bloodless complexion and gleaming cold eyes of the General, surrounded by all those soldiers with that exact same pallor.

Rintaro silently watched Nanami's reaction for a few moments before going on.

"I think you must have a clearer picture than I do of what's happening," he said, before dropping his gaze to the contents of his teacup. "It's not necessarily true that a person's perspective widens with age. We need to see things with our heart as well as our mind, but that view can easily become clouded. We might treasure a book when we're a child, then as time passes, we gradually forget it. We lose sight of a lot of important things, thinking that we are lighter for it."

"Has this happened to you, too, Rintaro-san?"

"I try to take care that it doesn't, but it doesn't always work out the way I intend. Especially in my line of work. I hear things like 'only the bestselling books are masterpieces,' or 'you're only a great writer if you make money' . . . Before I know it, I find myself falling into the trap of believing that kind of twisted logic."

Into Rintaro's gentle smile crept a touch of bitterness. It made him seem older. For a moment, Nanami saw the reflection of her own father's face.

"But you came," he said, looking up from his cup.

"Me?"

"Well, it's a bit of an exaggeration to claim I was waiting for you personally, but I was definitely hoping and waiting for someone like you to come along."

Rintaro placed his cup back on the desk and turned to look over his shoulder.

"Isn't that right, partner?"

Nanami gasped.

The back wall of the shop, which until moments earlier had been a solid wooden wall, was now bathed in a soft blue light. And silhouetted against that light sat a haughty-looking tabby.

The cat was undoubtedly the one Nanami had met a week earlier. The pointy ears in the exact shape of isosceles triangles, the jade-green eyes, and the perfectly horizontal silver whiskers were just as she remembered them.

"It's a pleasure to meet you again, Nanami."

The deep, rich voice was also exactly as she remembered it. She automatically started to get to her feet, but the cat gently shook its head as it stepped out of the light.

"Please don't bother. Keep your seat. It really isn't the right moment for you to go off on a sprint."

Nanami smiled with relief.

"I'm so glad to see you. I was afraid that it was all a dream and I was never going to see you again."

"Unfortunately, it was no dream. And not a happy one either." The cat sighed. "I must apologize for putting you in danger. For that, I'm truly sorry."

"Not at all. I was the one who asked you to take me."

Nanami put it like that; although, in truth, rather than ask, she had grabbed the cat by the scruff of its neck and threatened to dangle it that way forever. She was just grateful that it wasn't holding a grudge against her.

The cat had come right up to Nanami's feet. She leaned down to address it.

"What is this about you both waiting for me to come along?"

"Let's not jump to conclusions."

The cat's jade eyes glinted.

"It is true that I've been hoping to meet a young person with a strong spirit. I need their help to get back the books that have been stolen. However, I never said that you were that person."

At that point Rintaro interrupted. "I see you're as contrary as ever."

The cat turned its gaze to the bookseller.

"Mr. Proprietor, I'm not going to get the girl mixed up in this affair so easily. This time, our opponent is a dweller of a very different world to ours. And the amount of power he possesses is terrifying. I can't predict what might happen."

"Surely you're not going to stand by and watch those books disappear one by one?" Rintaro argued.

The cat's expression changed. Its eyes were piercing.

"Look, this girl's spirit is exceptionally strong. But it's not enough to be strong. To grab those books by force and try to escape from that labyrinth is nothing short of reckless."

"But that's exactly how she managed to get one of the books out, whereas I believe you've failed to get a single book back up to now."

Rintaro's words appeared to silence the cat.

"There are things you can't overcome by logic and reasoning," Rintaro went on. "I think Nanami sees that. I believe that's the kind of approach we need to take with an opponent of this caliber."

It was a low-key kind of face-off. Although the expression on the cat's face was severe, it didn't put its feelings into words. By contrast, Rintaro looked straight back and expressed all his thoughts without reservation.

"I think she has a lot more to offer than her bravery."

"Yes, I agree. She's an intelligent and truly courageous girl. I wish I could introduce her to a certain gutless, gloomy high school boy from ten years ago."

"I have no response to that," said Rintaro with a grimace, and the cat snorted with laughter.

Nanami couldn't follow the whole conversation, but she could tell that, despite the tension between them, there was a warmth, and an unshakable sense of mutual trust. She felt a little embarrassed to hear the two of them discussing her so earnestly. For a while she listened and observed, her hands clasped around the warm teacup. Then, taking a sip, she turned to the cat.

"And yet, you came back here to meet me. It means there's something I can do for you, right?"

"You're quite something, aren't you?" said the cat, somewhat taken aback. "After all you went through in part one, you're back and excited for the sequel."

"Once I start a story, I always read it through to the end. Scary books, difficult books, you never know what's written there unless you read the whole thing. Most importantly, if we just let this go, aren't they going to go on taking more and more books?"

"That's what the Gray Man known as the General intends. He has declared that it's necessary."

"And that's not all. There are still so many books in that castle that he's already stolen."

"Are you really thinking of trying to get them all back?" asked the cat.

"That's what I'm prepared to do."

Nanami picked up her oversize leather shoulder bag and pulled out a book. It was the old, worn volume that she had escaped with a week ago: *The Hollow Needle*.

The cat stared at it without commenting. Rintaro also sipped his tea without a word. After a few moments of silence, the cat finally opened its mouth.

"How come you're so brave?"

It was Nanami's turn to ponder awhile.

"I mean you can just borrow whatever you like from Natsuki Books," the cat continued, "read to your heart's content, and forget about everything else. Nobody would blame you for that. What's more, you'll never have to listen to another of the General's obnoxious speeches ever again."

"And no more creepy soldiers with muskets chasing me?"

"That's right."

"Absolutely not. I have to go back there again."

The cat's eyes narrowed at her determined tone.

"And why's that?"

"I don't know how to explain. I guess the best way to say it is that if I ignore everything that's happening, I'm going to regret it later. I've given up on so many things in my life so far, but I'm not going to give up on this, the thing that matters the most."

"The thing that matters the most?"

Nanami nodded and gently placed her hand on *The Hollow Needle* in front of her. It was a book she had read over and over while sitting home alone. She was familiar even with the way it felt to the touch. To Nanami it was much more than a bundle of pages—it was a precious friend that had supported her through the loneliest of times.

"I told you, I never forget a precious book."

And in that moment, the bluish whiteness that lit the aisle of the bookshop intensified. The whole shop became brighter, and Nanami had to squint in the dazzling glare. The cat was no more than a silhouette against the brightness.

"It looks as if I do need your help," said the cat in its rich voice. In the flickering light, its whiskers sparkled as if made of pure silver. "Will you accompany me?"

"Of course."

"The enemy is big, you are small. I can only warn you once again—there's danger ahead."

"And my answer is still the same—I can handle this."

"Fine words," remarked the cat, "but you know that they are fatally flawed if without evidence."

"I can handle that too. 'Hope made a show of reviving—not with any reason to back it, but only because it is its nature to revive.'"

The cat's eyes grew slightly rounder. From his seat next to Nanami, Rintaro laughed.

"*The Adventures of Tom Sawyer*? Nice quote."

"Yes, I really like that quotation," said the cat. "It's no innocent, naive work. At its core it's steeped in sorrow."

"But," retorted Nanami at once, "surely there's as much tenderness as there is sadness in the book."

"I see... You may be right," said the cat shortly, and it then turned to Rintaro.

"It doesn't look as if you'll be able to join us, Mr. Proprietor."

Nanami was surprised to see Rintaro nod.

"You can't come with us?" she asked him.

"Look at the passageway," he replied, pointing along the aisle between the bookshelves.

Nanami saw what he meant. The passageway at the end of the bookshop was much smaller than the last time she'd seen it. Although it was wide enough for a person to pass through, it was barely higher than the top of Nanami's head. It would be extremely difficult for a full-grown adult to pass through. In other words, it was way too low for someone of Rintaro's height.

"The books' power is getting weaker," Rintaro explained. "I might be able to force my way through, but I'm sure that's not the right approach. Brute force doesn't solve anything. It just masquerades as the solution."

He got up from his leaning position against the bookcase and knelt down in front of Nanami. This way, he was looking up at her face.

"Don't worry. If I'm needed, a way will open up again for me to come to help."

"Like last time?"

"That's right."

Nanami was sure it would.

"And, Nanami? Never forget that at the other end of that passageway, truth and the power of the heart are what matter most. And it's not of the slightest importance that you have asthma."

Rintaro threw the cat a glance.

"Nor does it matter that your companion is always so grumpy."

Nanami laughed out loud. Then she drained her cup of warm tea, got up from her chair, and walked over to join the cat. When she turned back to look at Rintaro, she saw him waving to them from under the soft light of the bookshop lamp.

Nanami took a deep breath and called out in a loud voice.

"Well then, we're off."

And with that, the blue light grew even stronger, enveloping the girl and the cat.

Nanami still had memory fragments of the day she first went to the library with her father.

She was yet to start elementary school, and back in those days her father would finish work in the early afternoon, then pick her up from day care. He'd always had a love for books and would read to Nanami every evening after dinner. One day, telling her it was time to go and search for new books, he took her to the library on the way home from day care.

Nanami was overawed by the imposing appearance of that massive building in the center of town, which seemed to crouch silently in wait. But when she stepped inside and took it all in, her eyes grew wide and she was left speechless. The high ceiling and vast floor space; the rows of shelves filled with countless books; finally, its unique air of silence and the faint smell of aged paper.

Everything was new to her. For a girl who couldn't run and

play in the park because of her asthma, the size of this space was wonder enough; she was soon to learn that the world it opened to her was more vast than she could ever imagine.

She read *Moko Moko Moko* by Shuntarō Tanikawa over and over, memorizing the whole book. *Frederick*, a picture book about a field mouse, she loved so much that some nights she'd even take it to bed with her. She never tired of looking at the slightly shy smile of the little mouse poet. Tales of a ladder to the moon, Santa Claus delivering presents in the cold of winter, and the mildly scary ghost story *Nenai ko dare da* were all tales she encountered at the library.

"The library again?"

Nanami's father was astonished when every few days his daughter would beg to visit. Then, sitting in the car on their way home from day care, his expression would quickly turn to a smile, and he would head that way.

At the library there was one elderly man with a white beard who always greeted his little asthmatic customer with a solemn expression on his face.

"Are you planning to read every book in this library?" old Mr. Hamura the librarian would say without even a hint of a smile, as he watched Nanami devour picture books one after the other.

At first, Nanami imagined him to be some kind of evil wizard from the dungeon of an ancient castle, and she would hide behind her father. But gradually she noticed that there was a kind of gentle light in the wizard's eyes. On holidays when Nanami and her father were sitting in one of the window seats reading, the white-bearded wizard would saunter over and casually leave a new book on the edge of their desk.

Her first encounters with *The Happy Prince* and *The Wonderful Wizard of Oz* were thanks to the librarian's efforts. And as she got older, Mr. Hamura would introduce her to books such as *Charlie and the Chocolate Factory* and *Bokensha-tachi*; later *Anne of Green Gables* and *Sherlock Holmes: The Complete Collection*. And it was also around this time that Nanami first encountered the *Arsène Lupin, Gentleman Thief* mysteries.

She was in sixth grade at elementary school when she first picked up *The Three Musketeers* and the rest of Dumas's D'Artagnan series. Nanami became so absorbed in this lengthy work, which ran to over ten volumes in its Japanese translation, that the beautiful flag of the musketeers with its white cross on a blue background began to creep into her dreams at night, along with the exploits of Athos, Aramis, and Porthos.

As she continued to visit the library, Nanami's world expanded. That wasn't all. Books had the power to lift her spirits, to rescue her from loneliness and sadness.

Even though she was in elementary school, because of her health issues, Nanami was never strong enough to play outside with friends. Her father got steadily busier at work and didn't have as much time as before to take her to the library. When Nanami got home from school she was greeted by an empty house and long hours spent alone. She managed to get through those dark evening hours thanks to reading. She wasn't sure if that was the right way to deal with things; what was certain was that books were her companions and their heroes taught her many things.

From the three musketeers, she learned how to have courage in the face of adversity.

From the Wizard of Earthsea, integrity and perseverance.

From Captain Ahab and Phileas Fogg, her indomitable spirit.

From the famous detective and the master phantom thief Arsène Lupin, compassion and humor.

And from all the books together, the habit of keeping hope in her bag along with her asthma medicine.

And now, thought Nanami, it was her turn to save those books.

Beyond the pale blue light stood the towering stone castle. Nanami shaded her eyes with her hand and examined it in detail.

She felt an odd sense of unease as she realized that its appearance had changed. Was it her imagination, or were the walls built up higher than before? And there seemed to be more of the gray flags fluttering in the wind, and even more gray-faced soldiers lined up beneath them. Previously, only a few soldiers had been scattered about on the battlements, but now there were definitely more of them, including a whole platoon that appeared to be patrolling the walls. Beyond, there were several towering spires.

"They got even stronger," muttered the cat to itself.

"Even stronger . . . ?" echoed Nanami, her hand still at her forehead. "You mean the castle gets bigger every time you come?"

"That's right. It wasn't so obvious before," said the cat bitterly. "It was a very gradual change. But now they're visibly gathering strength."

"What are we going to do? We only just got out of here the other day. How are we going to get into a castle that's even more secure?"

"There are two ways. Enter through the gate or jump over those walls."

"That's your way of telling me that you haven't given it any thought?"

"Well, humor is important when things get tough," the cat informed her grimly, before setting off straight for the gate. "I think that one has started to take an interest in you, so I don't believe he's going to fire shots at us right here."

"What if they do shoot at us?"

"Then . . ." The cat looked up at the castle walls. "We'll both try to run as fast as we can, like before."

The cat was right. No one opened fire on the pair. The ashen-faced soldiers on either side of the drawbridge remained expressionless and merely saluted as before.

"They're letting us in."

"That's the most important thing."

They passed through the gate with no interaction with the guards and found the interior of the castle had undergone considerable changes.

The bare and dusty pathway was now neatly paved with flagstones, along which a band of gray soldiers was marching at a brisk pace. As before, they all had the same blank face. The soldiers moving toward the castle donjon were empty-handed; those emerging from the building were carrying large crates. They were clearly transporting something from the castle, but they didn't say a word to one another as they worked, which meant that all that could be heard was the rather eerie sound of footsteps on flagstones.

Nanami and the cat arrived in the central courtyard to find there was no longer a fire burning on the altar in the center. The flames had been extinguished and nothing remained but piles of ash.

"Looks like they stopped burning books," Nanami remarked.

"Well, that's good news at least. If I'd found anyone was still committing such an act of barbarism, I was going to sneak up behind them and push them into the fire."

"Was that humor too?"

The cat didn't reply. Instead, it turned its attention to the stairway leading up to the donjon, from where the soldiers were bringing the wooden crates.

Nanami and the cat exchanged a quick glance, then started off across the courtyard toward the staircase. The line of crate-carrying soldiers continued to stream out, accompanied by a noise that seemed to come from deep within—a kind of muffled rumbling sound.

"I didn't hear that last time," said Nanami.

"Right. It sounds like some kind of heavy machinery."

As they climbed the stone steps, the dull sound became clearer. Just as the cat had suggested, it was as if some sort of factory was in operation somewhere within the building. When they got to the top, they peered in through the doorway to see at the far end of the red carpet the door to the General's Grand Hall standing open and unguarded.

Nanami stopped for a moment to regulate her breathing, then stepped onto the carpet and strode purposefully toward the door. She peered into the hall and let out a gasp.

"What happened here?"

The Grand Hall looked nothing like before. All the guards lined up along the walls had disappeared; in fact, there wasn't a soul to be seen. More than half of the candles in the glittering chandeliers had gone out, and the room was dim and gloomy. There were still two rows of polished white marble tables on either side of the carpet for displaying books; despite the General's supposed attachment to those books, now they lay there as if someone had casually tossed them onto the tables, and some had even fallen to the floor. *Treasure Island*, *My Father's Dragon*, and the remainder of the Lupin series were lying abandoned like unsold, secondhand books.

"That's odd," the cat muttered.

Just at that moment, a soldier carrying a wooden crate appeared from the far end of the hall. Nanami stiffened in anticipation, but the soldier passed by without showing the slightest interest in the pair.

Nanami looked in the direction the soldier had come from, and she frowned. At the far end of the hall, where once a luxurious velvet armchair had been positioned, she spotted a door that hadn't been there before. The door was guarded and seemed to be where the crate-bearing soldiers were emerging from. The mechanical noise was also coming from the other side of it.

"There must be more books behind that door," said the cat. "We have to go and see."

"But these books are just lying here. We have the option of grabbing them and running away."

"Do we really?"

The cat caught Nanami's meaningful smile and stopped for a moment, as if at a loss for words. Then it sighed.

"You've got a lot of guts," it remarked, setting off.

As the two companions approached the door, the monotone voices of the guards were raised in chorus.

"Who goes there? This is the Office of the Prime Minister."

"We're here to meet the minister," responded the cat calmly.

The guard clicked his heels and straightened his posture.

"Visitors for His Excellency the Prime Minister!"

And then, despite there being no sign of anyone around, voices came out of nowhere one after the other: "Visitors for His Excellency the Prime Minister! Visitors for His Excellency the Prime Minister!"

The door began to open slowly. And with it came a diabolical din that made Nanami flinch and, along with it, the smell of metal and grease. Nanami's eyes widened at the sight being revealed before her eyes.

A multitude of steel machines were haphazardly arranged,

almost on top of each other. The atmosphere was of utter disorder. Through the center ran the red carpet, but in here it was smeared with soot and grease and had become no more than a grubby pathway between the machines. On either side of it towered rotating pulleys, grinding gears, and pumping pistons, each of their vertical movements emitting great bursts of steam.

They were no longer in a castle. This was a factory.

Gray soldiers moved around in silence. Nanami looked closely and saw white sheets of paper gliding between interlocking black steel objects. As these papers passed through the machines, they gradually turned into thicker and thicker bundles, then were spun around, cut, pressed, and finally spat out onto a conveyor belt as fully bound books. The soldiers were steadily packing these books into wooden crates and then carrying them out through the door.

At the far end of the grimy carpet stood a slender, slightly built man in a gray suit and matching gray deerstalker cap, apparently overseeing the soldiers' work. As Nanami and the cat approached, he made a graceful turn to face them.

"How unusual for us to have visitors," he said with a cheerful laugh. He was a young man with gentle features. He resembled the gray-suited General, but the difference was that there was a trace of a smile on this bloodless face.

The young man doffed his cap and bowed deeply.

"Welcome to the Office of the Prime Minister."

His voice was entirely free of any malice; in fact, he seemed almost innocent, with a hint of boyish charm. He was a complete contrast to the pompous General.

"So, after the General comes the Prime Minister?" asked the cat, unable to hide its bewilderment. The Prime Minister watched the feline, his smile unwavering.

"I never expected you to come back. You must be quite the thrill seekers to return after such a terrifying experience last time."

"Do you know us?"

The Prime Minister laughed at Nanami's question.

"After the rampage you went on last time, everybody knows who you are. 'The Great Adventure of the Girl and the Cat,' what a wonderful tale."

The gray minister seemed to be enjoying the conversation; as he spoke, he turned around and headed down the dirty carpet toward the far end of the factory. At the end of the carpeted aisle was a black leather sofa with a polished sheen that was out of place in such a grimy environment.

The Prime Minister settled himself comfortably on the sofa and crossed his long, skinny legs.

"So, you're not satisfied with that one volume you took the other day; you're back for the rest of them, are you?"

"It's not a case of being satisfied or dissatisfied. That was a library book."

"I see. Well, go ahead and take them, then. They were all still there in the General's Grand Hall, right? There aren't any books you'd want here in this room."

"Just go ahead and take them?" the cat asked cautiously. "After all that previous obsession with them?"

"It was the General who was obsessed with those books,

not me. I've decided that I don't need them anymore. The bigger issue is you two showing up here. Your presence disturbs the soldiers, and if they stop listening to orders, it's going to be a problem for me."

He shrugged and made a dismissive gesture with his hand.

"You don't need to worry. I've no plans to collect any more books. You saw the courtyard? We've stopped burning books. The General's way was far too time-consuming and labor-intensive. I've adopted a brand-new system."

As if to punctuate the minister's explanation, a nearby machine let out a flamboyant gush of steam.

Nanami and the cat were both finding it difficult to keep up with the rather rapid developments of the story, but as they listened to the Prime Minister speak, they began to feel as if things might have been resolved.

Hesitantly, Nanami opened her mouth.

"What do you mean when you say you've adopted a brand-new system?"

"Our aim is to keep people away from dangerous books. And how can we achieve this? The General traveled around the world hunting out dangerous books, trying to gather them up one by one. That was totally impractical. Instead, we decided that it would be a far more effective approach if we ourselves produced a vast number of 'neo-books.' Then people will be entirely consumed by reading all these new books, leaving them no time to engage with any of that powerful literature. Thus, we accomplish what we set out to do."

He raised one skinny arm to indicate the machinery.

"This here is the bindery for those neo-books."

Once again, as if responding to the minister's speech, gears turned, conveyor belts shuddered, and the pistons made an odd sound. Then, with a head-splitting screech, the machinery began to spit out an even greater volume of books into the center of the massive room. There were so many that a large number of them overflowed the edges of the conveyor belt and scattered randomly here and there between the machines. In silence, gray soldiers gathered them up, packed them into crates, and carried them out.

Nanami picked up one of the books that had fallen by her feet and opened it. A puzzled expression crossed her face.

"It's blank."

It was true, the book was empty. Between the covers were nothing but blank white pages.

"Is this one of your 'neo-books'?"

"That's right."

"But there's nothing in it."

"Nothing in it? Yes, that's right. The content's unimportant."

Nanami was astounded.

"The key is quantity, not quality. We aim to completely fill people's lives with neo-books so that they won't bother with the older, dangerous books. You know how they say the best place to hide a tree is in a forest? Well, we figured the best place to hide a book is inside another book."

Nanami thought this had to be a joke, but the Prime Minister looked like a young child, excited to tell everyone his best idea.

"It's fine. As far as the books' content is concerned, all we need to do is what everyone's doing these days—list a bunch of easily understandable, stimulating, and provocative information repeatedly, and most readers will be hooked. Human beings just need some kind of stimulus in front of them to follow. As a result, everyone will avoid all those powerful books. Even if you take home those volumes of *Arsène Lupin, Gentleman Thief*, nobody will bother to pick them up."

His amused chuckle resounded through the room. Then, as if the joke was just too funny, he raised a hand to his mouth as if forcing back his laughter.

All the while, brand-new empty books were flying from the machines at a great pace. At times they were flung out so fast that the soldiers collecting them couldn't keep up, and they ended up strewn around the floor.

Nanami couldn't stop staring at the neo-book in her hand. Even though she didn't know for sure what was going on, she had spotted that there was something forced about the Prime Minister's cheerful demeanor. She decided it was time to uncover the truth.

"Why are you so afraid of books?" she demanded.

The Prime Minister froze, the smile still on his lips.

"Afraid?"

"You just said that books are dangerous to people. But it seems to me that you are simply afraid of them."

His expression didn't change; the smile was glued to his face.

"I'm not afraid of anything," he said through that unwavering smile. "I'm simply trying to eliminate things that are harmful to human beings."

"I've never heard of books being harmful," responded Nanami calmly. "My father used to tell me that books contain limitless worlds. Even if it's impossible for you to visit a place, a book can transport you there. And sometimes you come across a piece of old wisdom or an important thought that has almost been forgotten."

Nanami used to sit with her father in a sunny window seat and listen to him tell her these things. It was one of her happiest memories.

"And it's not all about knowledge or wisdom. He also explained how if you read a lot of stories, you become able to understand the feelings of many different people. That's the power of imagination, and it's one of the most important—"

"Imagination?!"

Nanami was interrupted by the high-pitched voice of the Prime Minister. Both she and the cat jumped at the sound. From the expression of horror on the minister's face you would have thought he'd been informed of an untimely death. He leaned toward the girl, his eyes bulging.

"But that's the worst evil of all!"

"Imagination is evil?"

"Of course. You understand absolutely nothing. Have you ever properly considered what imagination is?"

His tone—impatient and expecting no response—sounded like that of a schoolteacher berating a lazy pupil.

"Imagination is the ability to think about others. To put yourself in their shoes, to be able to sympathize with those weaker than oneself, to become someone who can occasionally offer a helping hand. That's the power of imagination."

"And what is dangerous about that?"

Nanami was genuinely astonished. The Prime Minister looked at her with pity in his eyes.

"I feel for you," he said. "You've really been taken in by the dangerous power of books."

This time he sounded as if he was consoling the same delinquent pupil.

"It's a dog-eat-dog world out there. Those with power kick those weaker than themselves to the ground, and then trample all over them. It's a new era where winner takes all. If you show too much kindness to others, someone will seize the opportunity to take advantage of you. In other words, imagination is a terrifying force that can only destroy your rich potential, Nanami."

Nanami shivered at the unexpected use of her name.

"How do you know my name?"

"Of course I know it. Didn't the General tell you? We're the ones who walk beside you."

The Prime Minister was still smiling, but now Nanami noticed that there was no warmth in that smile. It felt as empty as the General's grandiose speeches.

Did human beings really speak to each other this way? A chill ran down Nanami's spine.

"I've been walking beside people for a very long time now. I've observed so many winners and losers that I've lost count.

And I've seen how empathy and compassion render people helpless. Look at the successful people in the world. Not one of them has even a scrap of imagination. The thing they have in common is that they are determined to mow down other people without mercy. They are completely free from the power of books—in fact, they are the freest people in the world."

The Prime Minister leaned back again, his elbow resting on one arm of the sofa.

"What people need these days isn't the power of imagination; they need the power not to imagine."

His voice wasn't loud, but it seemed to brim with an eerie kind of pressure. As if in agreement with his sentiments, the machines began to whir ever faster, spitting out neo-books at a crazy speed. White shreds of paper whirled through the air like confetti on a wedding day.

"Be careful, Nanami!"

The sharp warning came from the cat at her feet.

"Don't be fooled by his outward appearance. His words are terrifyingly powerful."

"They seem to be." Nanami ran her tongue over her dry lips. "But he's got it all wrong."

"Not everything he says is wrong," replied the cat. "Perhaps what he's saying contains some important truths."

"I still think it's nonsense. He's making out that everyone in the world is fighting. But there are plenty of people who aren't."

As if to crush Nanami's voice, the machinery emitted an unpleasant earsplitting noise that rattled her whole head and made her want to plug her ears.

"Oh, there is so much that you've yet to learn," said the minister with an exaggerated sigh.

He settled back into his sofa.

"The most frightening aspect of today's competitive society is not the fierce cutthroat battles where people stop at nothing to win. It's the overwhelming force of the system that automatically labels anyone who refuses to participate in the competition as a loser."

"Overwhelming force?"

"Choosing not to fight, not to compete, doesn't mean you are exempt from competitive society. In today's world, there are no longer any exemptions. Nowadays, if you don't compete, you are automatically branded a loser. To put it another way, even choosing not to compete requires you to engage in a brutal struggle. It's an absurd contradiction. You have to see how dangerous the power of imagination must be in such a world."

The Prime Minister suddenly flashed a soft, conciliatory smile.

"But we don't want to get too lofty in our discussion," he said, his voice gradually dropping until it was no more than a whisper. "Why don't we stick to matters closer to home? Deep down, you must have realized that imagination just robs you of the strength to fight. You've lived your life constantly being considerate to others, which has meant having to endure so much. Can you honestly say that you're happy that way?"

"I put up with too much? Me?"

No one had ever said anything like this to Nanami; she was completely unsettled by it.

"That's right. Always holding yourself back, worrying that you might be inconveniencing the people around you. It must really cramp your style. And while you're putting up with all that, there you are being pushed further down and down to the bottom of the social ladder. I'll tell you this, no matter how much you care about and care for other people, they're not going to offer you any help in return. You should stop living such a confined life. Why don't you start living more freely? Go be true to yourself."

"Live more freely? Be true to myself?" Nanami repeated, mesmerized by the minister's words.

Yet, as she spoke, she felt something dark and heavy begin to stir deep in her chest. It swelled rapidly until it was all around her. Startled, she tried to brush it away with her hands, but without success. It continued to spread until she was completely enveloped. For a fleeting moment she heard a faint voice and caught a glimpse of the cat, then everything was swallowed by the darkness.

When her mind cleared, she was standing on a pitch-black plain.

"There's nothing I can do about it!"

From some distant place came the angry voice of her father. It was a familiar conversation.

"I'm sorry but I'm busy. I can't go to the library with you all the time."

And then there he was, standing in the gloom, his expression stern.

"I have to work as hard as I can so that we have enough

money to live. If I did everything you asked me, we wouldn't be able to eat."

As Nanami stood frozen in shock, a doctor in a white coat appeared in the distance. He walked up to join Nanami's father.

"You can't go calling an ambulance all the time for something so trivial."

Nanami remembered the scene from a night-time emergency room.

The doctor cast a cold glance at Nanami.

"I understand that you are concerned about your father, but you need to learn to take better care of your own health. You can't go using an ambulance as some sort of taxi."

As he came to the end of his speech, the doctor's features began to blur, and his face was transformed into that of a certain rather nervous elementary school teacher.

"Now, Nanami-chan, I know you don't want to inconvenience everyone else, so don't you think you should give this excursion a miss?"

A rigid smile on his face, the teacher continued in a condescending tone.

"Of course, I understand your feelings, Nanami-chan, but if for some reason you started to feel unwell during the excursion, it would cause trouble for everyone. I don't think you should force yourself to participate."

It wasn't only the school excursions.

She wasn't allowed to take part in sports day or use the school swimming pool. For everyone's sake. For everyone else . . .

Why only you?

The words seemed to fall from the sky and land somewhere behind her. Nanami spun around, but there was nobody there.

Why should you be the only one who can't join in?

The words were not being spoken by someone else. The voice was Nanami's own. She was about to reply that she had never thought about it that way, but her response was drowned out once more by her own voice.

Forget about other people. Start doing what you want.

If you put up with everything, you'll end up as other people's stepping-stone.

Nanami stood there in silence.

In that deep, deep darkness, with not one single bright spot, she stood and watched each word as it fell, and didn't move a muscle.

"You've been through so much, Nanami."

This time it was the Prime Minister's soft whisper that reached her ears.

"But isn't it enough now? If you keep thinking about other people, your own life will be ruined. Start living more freely. Be true to yourself."

Comforting words.

Start living more freely. Be true to yourself.

It felt to Nanami as if her body had become weightless and was beginning to float gently upward, then she took a breath and heard a faint sound in her chest. It was like a high-pitched whistle. She knew instantly that this was a bad sign, but there was nothing she could do about it right now.

The warning that it was dangerous to continue had somehow become entangled with the sweet, drowsy sensation that everything was just fine.

Then that balance was thrown by a sudden warmth that Nanami felt at her fingertips, spreading slowly upward through her hands and up into her arms, as if infusing them with light, and pushing the darkness back into her chest. She looked down at her fingers and saw there was light at their tips, and from somewhere beyond she heard the urgent voice of the cat.

"Nanami!"

She came back to her senses. Simultaneously all the strength drained from her body, and she fell to her knees.

"Nanami, are you all right?"

The cat's face was right there, serious and concerned. Nanami's breathing had turned ragged and there was a sickening wheezing coming from her lungs.

"You brought me back . . . thank you."

"Never mind thanks. Use your meds."

Nanami did as she was told, grabbing her inhaler from her pocket and taking a slow breath.

Nearby, the gears of the machinery kept on grinding, and steam spurted noisily into the air. Out of the corner of her eye, Nanami saw neo-books fly through the air and land on the floor with a thunk. It was hard to believe that a moment ago she had been standing in the all-enveloping peace of darkness.

"You look awful, Nanami," remarked the cat.

"I'll be okay . . . I think."

"You aren't convincing me. Your complexion is as gray as the Prime Minister's."

"That's a mean thing to say. Pretty hurtful to call me that creepy looking. It's true, though—I've rarely felt as bad as I do now."

She put her hand to her chest and took slow, careful breaths as she spoke.

"It felt as if I lost consciousness."

"You seemed to. But it was only for a short time."

Still kneeling, Nanami turned her attention to the sofa. The Prime Minister hadn't moved. He still sat there with his legs crossed, but his expression had changed. The cheerful smile was gone and the eyes that watched Nanami were emotionless.

"What a surprise. I didn't think you'd come back. Most humans do as I say."

"What the Prime Minister says is true," added the cat, shaking itself almost as if trembling. "That phrase, 'Start living more freely. Be true to yourself'—it has an appealing ring, but at the same time they're terrifying words."

Nanami noticed that the cat's face was tense with worry.

"You were calling my name the whole time, weren't you?" she said, reaching out an unsteady hand and gently stroking the cat's head.

Although the nightmare had only lasted a few moments, her forehead was covered in tiny beads of sweat, and her black hair was standing on end. Without bothering to wipe away the sweat, Nanami reached out with her right hand and pulled her bag closer.

"This book protected me."

"What book?"

She opened a corner of the bag to reveal *The Hollow Needle*, which was giving off a soft glow. In the chilling darkness, it was this book that had provided a reassuring warmth.

"You really are strong."

"It wasn't me. It was the book."

"No, you're the strong one."

The cat's tone was rough, but the warmth of its voice melted the chill in Nanami's chest.

"We shouldn't stay here any longer," the cat told her. "We don't have enough power."

"I'm fine."

"Nanami—"

"I can handle this. I was just a little spooked."

"Spooked?"

Nanami smiled a little grimly at the sight of the cat's perplexed expression. At the same time, she became aware that there were tears in the corners of her eyes.

"It seems that without realizing it, I've been dealing with a lot of stuff," she explained. "I thought I'd managed to cope with all of it in my own way, but I'm feeling a little defeated right now."

With a deep breath she wiped away her tears and sat up. She'd seen some unpleasant sights for sure, but at the same time she knew the voice she had heard wasn't truly her own. And if having the ability to recognize that was a sign of strength, then perhaps the cat was right about her after all.

"It's not a good thing to just behave however you like. People who commit violent acts always face a reckoning. I know that much."

"There aren't that many people who would agree with you. They lie without a second thought, commit fraud, hurt others, and then walk all over them. Perhaps society has become so distorted that it's impossible to survive without behaving that way."

"And that's why a lot of people take this guy at his word," said Nanami, placing both hands on the floor to lever herself slowly to her feet.

The Prime Minister continued to stare at Nanami, expressionless, his lips tightly closed.

"It doesn't sound too bad that phrase, 'Be true to yourself.' But if you think you can be true to yourself by kicking someone else to the gutter, then you've got it all wrong."

Nanami looked straight into the Prime Minister's eyes as she spoke. As she did so, an odd thing happened: the giant bookbinding machinery started to slow down; the pistons began to tremble and lose their rhythm; the steam jets weakened; and the gears that had up until now turned so smoothly began to shudder and creak. Even the soldiers running here and there came to a halt.

The Prime Minister spoke.

"How can you be so certain of that? Where does your confidence come from?"

"I'm not sure where it comes from. What I can say is that no matter how much I'd like to do whatever I want, there are many things I can't do without someone's help."

"I sympathize with you," said the Prime Minister, "but there are lots of people who don't require help. And I'm afraid to say that your fate is to be no more than a stepping-stone, trodden down by these people."

"That's not going to happen," said Nanami quietly.

The Prime Minister frowned. She ignored him and went on. "Whenever I'm having a hard time, plenty of people offer me help and support. The doctor encourages me and tells me not to worry too much; when I took the train, Itsuka was by my side. And as for journeying to this dangerous castle, this amazing cat came as my companion."

Nanami felt the cat stir, but she didn't glance down. She kept her eyes fixed on the face of the Prime Minister.

"My father told me a long time ago, 'We're not alone in this world. Whenever you're in trouble, there are lots of people you can ask for help. And then someday you will be able to repay that help.'"

These had been words of encouragement indeed for a girl who couldn't move as freely as she would have liked. In reality, Nanami wasn't sure if she could ever fully pay back what she owed other people. But, having experienced the difficulty of climbing a long flight of stairs, she knew she could never be someone who kicks another down. She would always prefer to be the one to reach out a hand so that they could walk up together.

Somehow the Prime Minister's expression had changed. His face was twisted as if in pain. It was a shock to Nanami to see such a reaction from a man who had previously appeared so relentlessly cheerful.

"How frustrating!" he said through clenched teeth. "I'm trying to give you advice. Guide you because I care about you. Can't you see that?"

"And I still want to know why you are so afraid of books."

"Afraid? Or . . ."

He sounded bitter, but unexpectedly didn't try to deny it. His face dropped and he supported his head in his two skinny hands as if he had a sudden migraine.

"Anyone with a heart ends up defeated. I've seen it with these very eyes. It's always the heartless ones who survive. The human heart is no more than ancient folklore now, remaining nowhere but in books. Well, it's even disappearing from their pages, too, these days. And that's fine, because that's how people become stronger."

The Prime Minister shook his head in irritation, a clump of his hair clutched in his hand.

"It's so obvious, yet still an unpleasant truth. Ugh. I feel sick."

With his left hand he began to scratch his head, causing his hair to stick up, and at the same time he snapped the fingers of his right. At once, the door marked "Office of the Prime Minister" burst open and hundreds of the soldiers who had previously been standing puppetlike around the castle rushed in, lining up on either side of the red carpet.

"Get out!" the Prime Minister shouted at Nanami. "You're making me ill."

Nanami was frozen in shock, so he continued to push her.

"Don't make me repeat myself. I think you'd better leave

before I lose my mind. If you make me any angrier than you have already, you won't be able to find your way home at all."

His eyes blazed with fury from between the fingers of his hands, now pressed up against his forehead.

Something had changed. Nanami sensed it—something shifting behind the figure of the Prime Minister. She had felt the same presence in the General's Great Hall before. A dark, sinister presence. She couldn't speak, couldn't move, as she felt a blackness surging forward from behind the Prime Minister who sat there in distress, head in hands. The blackness of it was breathtaking.

"This isn't good at all. Let's get out of here, Nanami."

The cat's commanding voice broke Nanami from her thoughts. Still, she couldn't tear her gaze from the direction of the sofa where the Prime Minister now writhed in agony.

"What's happening?" she asked.

"There's something inside that man. Or maybe that's actually his true form. Either way, we can't afford to hesitate."

"He seems to be in so much pain. How can we leave him like that?"

"I don't believe it!" the Prime Minister's trembling voice rang out. "Even in your current predicament you're still worried about me?"

On one side of his face, the Prime Minister was clenching his teeth in pain. But Nanami gasped when she saw the other side. There, he wore a thin smile, very different from the cheerful grin he'd presented since they first met. An icy grin.

"What a fascinating girl you are."

The tone of his voice was also completely different from before.

"Wh-who are you?" Nanami stuttered.

"That's a good question," he said through his icy smile. It was no longer a young person's voice; it had the timbre of a more mature man. "I'm the one who was created. Created by the hands of you human beings . . . How rare to actually meet a human being who still possesses such a heart . . ."

As he spoke, the door to the Prime Minister's Office slowly began to close again.

"Should I let you go, or should I make you stay . . . ? What a dilemma."

The cat called out urgently to Nanami, then spun around and dashed for the exit. Nanami followed right behind. Beyond the Prime Minister's Office was the General's Grand Hall, which was completely deserted. Instinctively, Nanami made for the nearest of the white marble cubes and grabbed the rest of the Lupin collection. As she was tossing the books into her shoulder bag, she glanced back to see the young gray minister cowering on the sofa. Over his head, an unidentifiable entity was growing. There was nothing to do but stop thinking and run.

Nanami and the cat walked silently along the blue-lit passageway. They didn't exchange any words. It wasn't relief for their safe return that had silenced them, more that the strange scene they had witnessed was weighing on their minds.

"Just a little farther," said the cat suddenly. "Can you make it?"

Nanami nodded. Her shoulder bag was stuffed to the brim.

"Are the books heavy?"

"I'm okay. I put quite a few in here but they're not heavy at all."

The bag contained *The Hollow Needle* and all its sequels—ten volumes in all—but Nanami barely noticed their weight.

"Here, physical strength counts for nothing," the cat reminded her. "All the strength that matters comes from the heart."

"He had a very strong heart too."

"Who? You mean the Prime Minister?"

"And yet he was suffering. He looked as if he was lost."

"In what way, lost?"

"I didn't really understand but in one of my favorite books I once read, 'All the ones who can't find their way back try sooner or later to become Emperor.' I wonder if the General and the Prime Minister somehow lost their way."

The cat didn't respond to Nanami's musings.

After they'd walked a while longer, the cat finally spoke up in its usual nonchalant tone.

"Anyway, at least you made it back. To be honest, there was a moment there where I thought you might not, yet you managed to keep up the dialogue right to the end and got that man to open the door for us. That was a significant victory."

"Are you complimenting me?" Nanami asked, with a half-hearted laugh. "I wasn't all that great. I couldn't understand even half of what he was saying."

"That's fine," said the cat without slowing its pace in the slightest. "You can't express everything with words. If you really analyze conversation, what you are conveying when you're talking isn't the meaning of your words, rather it's your will to convey them. If you express how you feel from your heart, then the content and meaning will follow. However, in today's world such accepted truths have come crashing down. People stack up their cold, heartless words in perfect rows like bricks and label them logic, believing that as long as something is logical, the message will automatically be conveyed. Still, a cold glass of logic can't compare to a nice warm cup of tea."

"It's curious," said Nanami, staring at the figure of the cat walking in front. "You are talking about really difficult concepts, but I completely understand what you're saying."

"That's because I'm sincere about conveying it to you. You mustn't forget that words are like a telescope. They help you see the things you want to see, but they leave you blind to everything else. In that sense, the Prime Minister cunningly used clever words to grab your attention and draw you in, conveniently making the rest invisible to you. But you outsmarted him by never forgetting about the world outside the lens."

"As I said just now, I'm not all that special. I've caused a great deal of inconvenience to many people in my life. It was just that I couldn't agree with what he was saying. Maybe I'm just too cynical."

As they talked, the light in the passageway grew brighter.

Nanami had just experienced something utterly terrifying, but gradually her fear had eased off. The cat's soothing voice seemed to have that effect on her.

"I guess this is goodbye again," she said, squinting against the glare of the light.

"I suppose it must be."

"When's the next quest?"

The cat looked momentarily thrown, then continued in its usual detached tone.

"That's a strange question. You managed to get your beloved Lupin collection back. And the Prime Minister told us that he didn't plan to steal any more books. Do we need to go on another quest?"

"I do get it, you know. I know perfectly well that things aren't over."

The cat stopped walking but didn't look back.

"I see . . ."

Then, in the steadily intensifying glow, it turned its whole body around to face Nanami.

"Well, with you around, maybe we can manage something."

Its green eyes shone with wisdom.

"Manage something?"

"You are quite right that this isn't over yet. The Gray Man has to be stopped."

The last part came from far away, as if even the cat's voice had been consumed by the light.

Nanami found herself standing in a corridor with a

gleaming wooden floor, lined with wooden bookshelves full of secondhand books. Cast-iron lamps hung overhead.

At the end of the long aisle sat Rintaro, patiently waiting.

Nanami had never seen her father, Seiichiro, so furious. As far as she was concerned, her father could be strict with her, but he wasn't easily angered. Most of the time he was calm and patient. Nanami figured that it was because of these very personality traits that he always ended up working too hard.

Now he was beside himself with fury.

She hadn't even gotten home late—it was just after midday.

It was not the time she got back that Seiichiro had a problem with, although he had probably started to worry more than ever since she'd returned late the other day. It was the realization that the daughter he had trusted to travel exclusively between home, school, and the library might in fact be sneaking around behind his back.

Nanami had left early in the morning and, after a few hours, when she hadn't come home, Seiichiro had called Itsuka's house. That was how he'd learned that Itsuka wasn't out with Nanami—she was participating in an archery tournament.

So where was Nanami? She'd lied about being with her friend. Why had she become so secretive lately?

Seiichiro scowled at his daughter. Nanami had come home

alone by train from Natsuki Books, but the fact she had taken on such a challenge simply doubled her father's anger.

"You can't do things like that, Nanami. You're just not strong enough."

They sat across from each other at the kitchen table. Seiichiro's exasperated voice dominated the small space.

"It's fine to go to the library, or to go out sometimes with your friend. But lying to your father and taking the train to somewhere far away is simply unacceptable."

"I'm sorry."

There was nothing for Nanami to do except offer a genuine apology.

"Look, I'm really busy at work. Please don't cause me any more worry."

"I'll take care—"

Nanami kept her head lowered and her eyes fixed on the tabletop. She dropped her voice a little.

"Do you think it might be possible for you to work shorter hours?"

"What did you say?"

Nanami was startled to be met by such a tone of disbelief.

"The world is tougher than you think. It doesn't matter how hard you work, life doesn't get easier. And if we don't have money, I can't afford to send you to university. These days, if you're not careful, you'll find yourself kicked to the bottom of the social ladder."

A sense of discomfort began to stir inside Nanami, but her father didn't seem to notice.

"You're already in the second year of junior high," he went on. "This is no longer the time in your life to be going to the library every day to read books. You ought to be more focused on your future. When you go out into society, you'll have to struggle by yourself to survive. Nobody's going to help you."

Nanami couldn't believe that her father, who had once loved books so much, could be saying things like this. All at once she realized why she was feeling that discomfort.

At times her father sounded just like the Gray General or the Prime Minister. He was nothing like either of those men, and yet some of the things he was saying she'd previously heard from them: *kicked to the bottom of the social ladder . . . you have to survive . . . nobody will help you.*

Deciding she must just be overtired, she lifted her head and was horrified by what she saw. Her father's complexion looked gray. It couldn't be, but there it was—a face with all the blood drained away. A gray face.

There was a thumping sound in Nanami's chest, and suddenly she found it difficult to breathe.

"What is it? . . . Nanami?" asked Seiichiro, his voice full of concern.

Nanami found she couldn't look him full in the face anymore.

"Are you having an asthma attack? Quick, use your inhaler!"

Nanami didn't need to be told; she was already pulling it from her pocket and gulping down its contents.

"Clearly you pushed yourself too hard today," said her father. "Where on earth did you go, and what were you doing?"

Seiichiro's voice seemed to come from somewhere in the distance. Nanami reached up and put her hand to her neck. She'd broken out in a cold sweat. She adjusted her gaze slightly and, all of a sudden, thought she caught sight of something in the gloom of the kitchen—a gray suit.

The one who walks beside you . . . The one who was created . . .

She didn't know what these words meant.

But they weren't from some story set in an alternative world far, far away; the gray men were right there with them.

And with that thought, she felt as if something was being sucked from her body. Overcome with dizziness, she collapsed forward onto the table.

THE ONE WHO PRO-LIFERATES

It was the first fever Nanami had had in a long time.

She lay on her bed, thoroughly bored by the sight of the ceiling. She'd been there ever since the afternoon she'd come home by train from Natsuki Books.

Perhaps she'd just been exhausted after her stressful journey. But, while her father was raging, her mind had seemed to relax somehow—although that might not have been the right word—and she had simply passed out.

Her father explained to her afterward that although she had a fever, there was no asthma attack and he hadn't needed to call an ambulance. He'd been so shaken by the incident that all his anger had immediately melted away, and he'd carried her to bed to get some rest.

She recalled dozing and, in between, she had fragments of memory: the sky turning red outside, the sun setting, and her father by her side the whole time. When she finally opened her eyes, there was bright blue sky between the gap in the curtains.

"You did push yourself too hard after all," said Seiichiro with what sounded like a sigh of relief.

His expression was as stern as ever, but although Nanami could see he was tired from sitting with her all night, his gray complexion from the previous day was gone.

"What's wrong? Is there something on my face?" he asked.

Nanami hastily shook her head and tucked herself farther under the covers to avoid her father's eyes. However, she was relieved to see that the father she knew was back; a little bit strict but very sincere and full of concern for Nanami whenever she wasn't well.

Seiichiro had some thoughts about his daughter's situation. He was thinking how to put them into words.

"I'm not going to ask you to tell me where you were or what you were doing," he said eventually. "I understand that there are things you can't talk to your father about. Just don't do anything that is going to put a strain on you. I know you're aware that you're not physically strong."

Nanami poked the top of her head out from under her blankets and nodded.

"Promise?"

She nodded a second time.

It was then that Nanami glanced at the clock and realized it was already almost noon. But her father was still in his casual clothes. It was a pleasant change to see him without a suit and tie on a weekday afternoon.

"What about work?" she asked.

"I would never leave you here by yourself. I took the day off."

"A day off?"

"I'll worry about work again tomorrow. Today I'm going to be with you all day."

"Really?"

Nanami grinned with delight, but her father gave her a sharp look.

"Just so you know, it's not easy to take time off. I have so much to do. I really need to be back by tomorrow afternoon, so get well quickly."

Nanami mumbled a response and pulled the blankets back over her face. She didn't want her father to see that she was still smiling.

"Right then." Seiichiro sighed, getting up from his chair.

"Dad?" said Nanami, her voice deliberately subdued.

"What is it?"

"I'm sorry."

Seiichiro frowned a moment at this, then relaxed his shoulders and shook his head.

"No . . ." he said softly. "I think it may have been for the best after all."

He scratched his head and squinted in the daylight streaming in through the window.

"I've been too busy lately. I believed I was doing it for your benefit, but perhaps I took it too far."

This response took Nanami by surprise.

"But that doesn't mean you're forgiven for going off somewhere and lying to me about it. You're banned from going to the library until you're fully recovered."

"Okay," said Nanami obediently. "If I promise to stay home, can I go into your study?"

"Are you planning to read in bed?"

"Am I not allowed?"

"I'm not saying you can't, but—"

"Do you hate books now?"

The words just slipped out. At this moment, it felt as if she was close to her father for the first time in a long while. She peered at his puzzled face from behind her bedcovers.

"Well, yesterday you told me that I shouldn't be reading all the time," she persisted.

"Did I really say that?"

Seiichiro seemed genuinely confused.

"I guess I'm not the best at communicating. . . . All right, go ahead, use my study however you'd like."

"Really?"

"Remember—I know I keep saying it—please don't push yourself too hard. If you get another fever, I'm going to forbid you completely from reading."

"Okay," said Nanami again, making sure her expression was as serious as possible.

In truth, she didn't feel at all sick. It was a pity that she couldn't visit the library, but to take time off school and stay home reading as much as she liked was heaven. Even better, her father was staying home with her.

She curled up under the covers and enjoyed the warm feeling that spread through her.

Her father's study was not very big—only six tatami mats in size—but every wall was crammed with books. There was a small desk and chair in one corner, but as her father rarely worked from home, they felt irrelevant to the space.

That afternoon, Nanami entered the study and sat herself at the desk, from there she scanned the walls of books. As it was her father's study, many of the books were too challenging for Nanami. He worked for a brokerage company, so a section of the shelves was given over to books on economics and politics. However, the majority of the books were a diverse mix of literature, philosophy and ethics, and other non-work-related titles.

As she gazed at the impressive array, Nanami's mind kept returning to the mysterious events at the castle.

The bizarre gray figure of the Prime Minister was stuck in her head. His cheerful persona had peeled away, revealing a very raw frustration. In the end he had appeared to be suffering some sort of torment as he drove Nanami and the cat from the room.

She found herself looking now at one particular shelf. It was where they kept the picture books she had read as a child. In the far corner was the copy of *The Hollow Needle* that Nanami had rescued from the General's Grand Hall. Yesterday, she had also brought back the remaining nine volumes of the Lupin series, but the moment she stepped back into the Natsuki Books bookshop, they had instantly reverted to their original weight, and hung heavy on Nanami's shoulder. She'd decided to leave the books there and take only *The Hollow Needle* home with her. She intended to retrieve the others and return them to the library after she felt better.

However, she knew that this would not make the problem go away. There were still a great number of books in that Grand Hall and even more in other parts of the castle. She was certain of it.

And that wasn't all. The cat had said, *The Gray Man has to be stopped.*

Nanami pictured the surprisingly diminutive figure of the cat as it had walked away from her.

The one who walks beside you . . . The one who was created . . .

Two phrases that were really difficult to grasp.

Nanami had repeated them to Rintaro that day. He'd merely looked thoughtful and told her to give him some time to consider their meaning.

She made up her mind that when she was fully recovered, she was going to ask her father to take her to Natsuki Books; hopefully, Rintaro would help her come up with a plan. There was no way she was going to sneak out of the house again; this time she would get her father's help. The problem was how to explain the situation to him, but she felt that after the way they'd communicated this morning she'd manage somehow. One of Nanami's best attributes was her ability to look at things in a positive light.

"When I'm better I'm going to the bookshop," she announced, daringly, to herself.

Now that she'd made her decision, Nanami quickly switched gears. It was time to choose which book to read. Should she pick a thick novel that she'd never read before? Or would it be nice to look at one of her old picture books for the first time in a while? Even if she went to bed a little early tonight, she would still have loads of reading time tomorrow. And her father would be there with her until noon.

Before she knew it her face had relaxed into a huge smile.

In the middle of the night, Nanami's eyes suddenly popped open.

She'd slept late the previous morning, which meant that she probably hadn't been sleeping very deeply. She glanced at the clock and saw that it was about to turn midnight.

There was a strange unease in her stomach, which propelled her out of bed and to peer through the gap in the curtains. It had started to drizzle and was colder than it had been in the daytime. The scene outside was made even more miserable by the forlorn light from the flickering streetlamps.

Deciding to get a glass of water from the kitchen, Nanami went out into the corridor, then suddenly stopped. Leading down to the first floor was a staircase, at the bottom of which was her father's bedroom to the right, and beyond at the end of the hallway, his study. The study door was slightly ajar, and a faint light shone from inside. At first, she thought her father must still be up, but then she realized that the light wasn't the usual illumination from the overhead electric bulb. She crept down the stairs and gently pushed the door open. It was just as she had thought—the whole study was filled with that now-familiar bluish-white light. The bookshelves were glowing, almost swaying, as if tempting Nanami closer.

"How did this get here?" she asked aloud.

Stepping into the light, she expected to see the endless passageway. It wasn't there. Instead, all four walls of bookshelves glowed pale blue. The very brightest of all was the corner where Nanami had stored the library's copy of *The Hollow Needle*.

She stretched out a hand to touch the book and heard a familiar low voice.

"Sorry to disturb you at this hour, Nanami."

She spun around to see the tabby cat crouched under the bookcase on the opposite wall. The sudden appearance of Tiger the Tabby didn't really surprise her anymore, but she was taken aback by the cat's altered appearance. The triangular ears and jade-green eyes were the same as ever, but its fur was rough and tousled, its breathing was labored, and its face, usually so haughty and bold, looked haggard and exhausted.

"What happened to you?"

"The event I feared is about to take place. The Gray Man is about to make his master move."

Nanami immediately picked up on the urgency in the cat's voice. She knelt down and placed a hand on its back. A portion of its fur was black and scorched. Something unthinkable must have occurred to leave burn marks like these.

"What happened?"

"I don't have time to explain right now. I need your help."

This was the first time Nanami had been asked directly for her help.

"In ordinary circumstances I would never get you involved in something like this, but you are the only one who can stop that man."

"Who are you talking about? The General? The Prime Minister?"

"Neither of those two. Or, in a way, you could say both of them. The Gray Man embodies various human emotions. The General, the Prime Minister, these are only two dimensions of that being. Anyway, your presence seems to have been unexpected and he's now rushing to bring things to a conclusion."

The cat shook its head sorrowfully.

"I really hate to involve you in all this, Nanami, but there is nothing else left to do."

It looked Nanami straight in the eyes and repeated the request.

"I need your help."

"Of course," she replied without hesitation. Her voice rang out.

The cat's eyes widened at such a determined response and Nanami was caught in their stare. She frowned.

"Why do you seem so surprised?" she demanded.

"I'm not surprised. I was just reminded of something."

"Of what?"

"A long time ago there was a boy who came to my aid in the same way that you're doing. I used to think he was a hopeless, apathetic kid, yet he was willing to risk danger to help me. With a willing smile he offered me his help to protect books. His personality was vastly different from yours, but it's strange how much being with you now reminds me of him. I miss those times."

The cat's luminous eyes reflected deep emotion. It was a rare moment for this habitually composed animal who never expressed unnecessary sentiments.

Of course, Nanami couldn't know anything of the cat's memories. Still, she had an idea of the identity of the boy it was talking about.

"I'm definitely not as clever as that boy, and I'm physically weaker, too, but I'm determined not to lose to him on mental strength."

"Don't worry. Your mind is the most powerful weapon in that labyrinth. Why do you think we met back then in the library? It's become clear to me now that it was no coincidence. You have the power to save books, and that's why I was led to you."

"I always knew it wasn't a coincidence," replied Nanami with a small laugh.

The usually unfazed green eyes wavered slightly, and the cat slowly bowed its head.

"I deeply appreciate it."

For once, the cynical feline sounded totally sincere.

"So, what do we do now?" Nanami asked. "There's no magic passageway here."

"There is a path."

The cat indicated the bookshelf directly behind it. Nanami could now see that a passageway *was* there, but it was no more than a tiny opening between the lowest shelves of books, barely the height of the cat. It was the same as the previous passageways she'd encountered but on a far smaller scale. Even the slight Nanami would find it impossible to pass through.

"So tiny?"

"That's the limit at this location. The books' power is definitely weakening."

"Then what should we do?"

"The library."

Nanami looked horrified.

"Go to the library?"

"So many more books are still there. You remember the first passageway we took? It should still be wide enough. You remember the spot?"

"I remember, but don't you know what time it is?"

Nanami looked at the wall clock. As she expected it was already midnight.

"To get into the library we have to get through the front door, past reception," she protested. "There are all kinds of barriers. It's not open twenty-four hours a day, you know."

"That won't be a problem. We can get into the building."

Nanami was flabbergasted; the cat looked back unperturbed.

"You'll see when we get there. Do you doubt me?"

"A week or two ago I would definitely have had my doubts, but . . ."

She stopped and shook her head.

"Now I believe you."

"Splendid. Well, time is of the essence. Please get to the library as quickly as possible."

"Understood. I'm definitely coming; just be sure not to push yourself too hard alone."

Nanami took the cat's head between both hands. Predictably, its eyes grew wide.

She could see how her companion's whole demeanor had changed. It seemed barely present; it felt to Nanami that if she let go of the feline now, it might just dissolve into nothingness. Even though she had hold of its head, it didn't struggle at all. It continued to look her straight in the eyes.

"Just wait for me. Okay?"

The cat gave as much of a nod as it could, caught there between Nanami's palms.

"Nanami, who's there?"

The voice came from the hallway beyond the study door. It was her father.

The cat threw a glance in that direction, then swiftly turned away.

"I'll be waiting. You're our last hope."

It leapt into the tiny passageway at the very moment the study door opened. Nanami got to her feet as her father appeared around the door, wearing his pajamas.

The bluish light was gone, and the study's only illumination was the flickering streetlamp beyond the small window.

———

"What on earth are you doing here at this time of night?" asked Seiichiro, stifling a yawn.

He looked around curiously, but of course there was nothing out of the ordinary to be seen.

"And who were you talking to in the dark?"

He flipped the light switch, causing Nanami to screw up her eyes against the wash of brightness.

"I know you love books, but what are you doing getting out of bed in the middle of the night when you're not even fully recovered yet?"

"I'm sorry."

"And making all this noise by yourself in the dark . . . Well, it just isn't normal, Nanami."

The irritation in her father's voice made Nanami stiffen. He was right—none of this was normal. She knew that she wasn't normal. In fact, this past week, nothing normal had happened to her at all. A talking cat, glowing blue passageways of books, gray men . . . But just because they were all abnormal didn't mean that they weren't important.

Nanami stood in the middle of the study, her cheeks flushed and her lips pressed firmly together, looking back at her father.

"What is it, Nanami?"

"Dad, I have a favor to ask."

Seiichiro could sense that something was amiss with his daughter as she stood there in front of him, both hands clasped in front of her chest.

"What's wrong? Why are you so upset?"

"I know you're going to think I'm crazy, but I want to go to the library."

Seiichiro was thrown. For a moment he seemed desperately to be trying to make sense of things. He blinked a few times, then ventured a response.

"Of course, when you're fully recovered let's go together. It's been a while."

"By the time I'm fully recovered it'll be too late."

"Too late? You mean you want to go tomorrow?"

"Not tomorrow. Now."

Naturally, Seiichiro was speechless.

"I know it sounds as if I've lost my mind," Nanami continued, "but it's really urgent. I need to go to the library right now."

"Nanami . . ."

Seiichiro was still stunned. Somehow he managed to find some words.

"You know that's not possible. What are you talking about?"

"I know it's weird."

"Then at least explain to me what's going on. Without any details, asking to go to the library at midnight . . ."

"Of course I'll explain everything. But they told me there's no time. There's no time to stand around here and tell you all about it."

"Don't talk rubbish, Nanami!"

Seiichiro's voice turned sharper. The sleepiness was gone from his face, and now deep wrinkles were forming between his brows. His mood was switching between confusion and irritation.

"You know, you've been behaving very oddly lately. Lying to me, making me worry, and now getting up and making a scene in the middle of the night. You're causing me no end of problems. I admit I've been too busy at work lately, and I really am sorry about that. But there's acceptable behavior and then there's totally unacceptable."

"I know I've made you worry—"

"So, then if you know—"

"Someone has asked for my help."

Nanami's determined tone startled Seiichiro for a moment and he stopped talking.

Nanami knew what she was saying sounded absurd, and that it was totally understandable for her father to be angry. She was acting bizarrely. From his point of view, his asthmatic daughter had suddenly come home late, then traveled alone to a distant town, and now she was behaving strangely in his study in the middle of the night.

And yet . . .

She couldn't get the image of the cat out of her head—its haggard face, the urgent look in its eyes, and the burnt patches of fur on its body . . . She didn't know what was going on, but she knew it had to be something terrible.

"They told me they'd be waiting for me. A very good friend."

"A friend?"

"There are a lot of things that I don't understand, but I do know that my friend is asking for my help. Didn't you once tell me that if someone was in trouble I should be the kind of person who lends a hand?"

Seiichiro listened silently as his daughter did her best to convince him.

"You've always told me that. That we're not alone in this world. That we don't always realize it, but we live with the support of all sorts of different people. You said that I, especially with my delicate health, have relied on many people. And therefore, you told me that if I ever saw someone in need, I should be the kind of person who offers them support."

By the end of her speech, Nanami wasn't quite sure anymore what she was talking about. It had been a long time since her father had said those words. She wasn't even sure why they'd come into her head at this moment.

Her father stood and listened, a grim expression on his face; he didn't speak. After a long moment of silence, he looked up at the ceiling, then down at his feet; then he put his hand to his forehead and shook his head several times.

"Nanami?" he said, as if forcing out the words. "Stay where you are a minute."

"Dad—"

"Just don't move. Okay?" he shouted as he left the room.

Nanami remained standing alone in the empty study. Outside, the rain had become heavy. The library wasn't too far from the house, but it wouldn't be easy for her to walk there by herself in this weather. And, besides, her father would now be watching her.

You're our last hope.

The image of the cat saying this as it turned to leave was burned into her brain.

She bit her lip, as finally Seiichiro came back.

At first she'd assumed he was going to make her go back to bed. Instead, he was wearing his thick, down jacket and carrying Nanami's green coat.

"The library then," he said, as if forcing the words out. It was then that Nanami noticed something shiny in his other hand. He was holding the car keys.

"Are you sure you're feeling up to it?" he added.

Nanami was speechless at the change in her father's attitude.

"You're in a rush, right? So . . . better hurry."

"Dad?"

"It's raining out there so you'd better take your coat. And don't forget your inhaler."

Tears welled up in Nanami's eyes, distorting her vision of her father's face.

"Really, what a daughter . . ." said her father, shaking his head as if in despair. "Seriously, what a daughter," he mumbled over and over to himself, as he placed the coat around Nanami's shoulders.

In the car, Seiichiro said nothing. Even though he'd previously made so many demands for information, now there was no break in the silence.

It took less than five minutes to reach the library. There weren't any other cars on the dark, rainy road, and not a single pedestrian to be seen. As they pulled into the library's deserted car park and stopped under the portico in front, Nanami spotted a soft bluish light that seemed to start outside the main glass doors of the building entrance and make its way deep into the library. The pale, shimmering corridor of light was narrower than the one Nanami had seen at the bookshop. It looked barely wide enough for Nanami to pass through.

As soon as the car came to a stop, Nanami hurried to unbuckle her seat belt and put her arms through her coat sleeves.

"It doesn't look as if I'll be able to go with you," said Seiichiro from the driver's seat.

Nanami looked over at her father's face. The grim expression hadn't gone, but she could also read confusion, hesitation, and a host of other emotions. She wasn't sure if her father could see the same things that she did, but his eyes were fixed on the entrance to the library as he opened his mouth and spoke in careful, measured words.

"Normally parents don't bring their daughters to the library in the middle of the night, nor do they send them off with a big smile and a 'see you later.'"

Nanami had no response to that.

Her father stared at the raindrops on the windshield as if searching for something; then eventually he seemed to find it.

"We're not alone in this world," he whispered softly.

The same words Nanami had used when they were in the study.

"It's what your mother always used to say."

"Mum did?"

"I hadn't heard that phrase in a while. I don't know why you suddenly said it, but it was as if your mother was talking to me. As if she was telling me to listen to what you were saying."

Nanami scarcely dared to breathe as her father continued.

"Your mother suffered from poor health, yet she was always so cheerful. She always used to say that we weren't alone. That we live our lives supporting others, and being supported in return. That if you are going through a difficult time, you should reach out and ask for help. And whatever kindness is paid to you by others, you can always pay it back."

Nanami had never heard her father talk like this before. He didn't like to mention her mother, who had passed away at such a young age.

"These days you never hear people say things like that. They're always occupied with their own concerns, believing that they're the most important thing in their worlds. I hate to say it, but I think I'm just like them. You give me so much that is valuable every single day, and I had completely lost sight of that."

The rain couldn't reach the car as it sat under the large overhang in front of the library; it cascaded down the ornamental rain chain at the corner of the roof.

"The world is in constant flux, but there are some things that must never change. And many of those things are written about in books. That's why your mother and I used to say that we wanted you to read books from all over the world."

"Books from all over the world . . ."

"And that's why we gave you the name 'Nanami' meaning 'Seven Seas.' It's to symbolize the whole world."

Nanami couldn't speak. She hadn't expected to hear such a precious story at a time like this.

Raindrops splashed onto the leaves of the bushes lining the road, and they swayed as if performing a gentle waltz.

"Your mother wouldn't have hesitated to bring you here tonight," added Seiichiro with a wry smile. He turned to look at Nanami.

"Explain everything to me when you get back, okay?"

She nodded.

"Have you got a handkerchief and tissues with you?"

Nanami was slightly confused by the odd expression of concern, but she nodded again.

"And you have your inhaler?"

At this, a small laugh escaped Nanami's lips.

"It's just like going on a school field trip."

"How much easier this would all be if it were just a field trip . . ." Seiichiro sighed, his hands still gripping the steering wheel. "You'd better get going, then."

His voice trembled faintly.

"And please come back as soon as possible. I'll be waiting right here for you."

Nanami gave one final nod of her head and climbed out of the car. She turned to see her father get out of the driver's seat to stand next to the vehicle.

She clasped her hands together in a gesture of thanks.

"I'm off, then!" she called in the loudest voice she could muster.

She didn't wait for a reply before she turned and ran into the corridor of light.

As Nanami had observed, the corridor of light extended beyond the glass entrance doors. Then it was just as she'd predicted: it led past the reception desk on the first floor, up the staircase to the second floor, and straight to the French Literature bookshelf at the back. There she found the same bookcase-lined passageway that she and the cat had taken a week earlier.

Nanami didn't slow her pace for a moment, rushing on into the light. Strangely, although she was running with all her might, she didn't feel at all asthmatic. Eventually the passageway was enveloped in a dazzling light and, just as Nanami thought she had passed through to the end, she was confronted by a huge wall. It was a castle rampart.

This was vastly different from the castle walls she had seen before. It extended to the left and right seemingly without end. On the far side, many towering spires, large and small, gave the impression less of a castle and more of a giant fortress. Gray flags filled the whole space above the battlements, arranged so thickly that there was barely a sliver of light between them. Below them, an ominous row of black cannons.

But it wasn't the castle's imposing appearance that took Nanami's breath away. It was the smoke and flames.

The castle was on fire.

Heavy black smoke billowed into the air, and the expanse of sky was stained an eerie reddish black. Sultry gusts of wind carried with them the stink of burning.

Nanami stood there for a while without speaking, before turning her attention to the castle gate ahead of her. There on the drawbridge, backlit by the fiery red glow, stood Tiger the Tabby.

The cat said nothing to Nanami. Instead it turned and walked ahead of her through the castle gate.

Nanami crossed the drawbridge and entered the castle to

find herself in a labyrinth of walled flagstone pathways, all branching off at different angles. Without hesitating, the cat strode ahead into the maze.

From time to time the smell of smoke was carried on the hot wind, and Nanami heard the loud crack of something exploding. The noise seemed to get closer and then recede again. Columns of soldiers ran past them on both sides. Every one of them was completely expressionless, making it impossible to tell if they were panicking or perfectly at ease.

The castle walls were so high that Nanami and the cat couldn't see the flames that surrounded them, but it was obvious to the pair that just because the fire wasn't visible didn't mean that they were out of danger. The narrow sliver of red sky they could see above the walls was growing darker by the minute.

"What's going on?" Nanami asked.

"The Gray Man has started a fire," replied the cat. "He wants to burn down the entire castle."

It was hard to believe. Without turning to look at Nanami, the cat continued.

"He was going to take his time erasing books from the world. His plan was to steal books gradually so that hardly anybody would notice. It was the most reasonable approach, and also sure to succeed. Then circumstances changed. You showed up."

The cat ascended a short flight of stone steps and selected the center route out of three branching paths. Originating somewhere in the distance, a scorching wind blew past them.

"Many people have visited this castle over the years. And most of them were captivated by the Gray Man and chose to 'live more freely and be true to themselves,' as he put it."

"In other words, they forgot about books?"

"That's right. And many of those people who forgot about books went back into the real world and achieved great success. People who abandoned their books lost the power of their imagination; they used relentless aggression to deceive, exploit, and plunder others, hoisting the flag of 'free will' above their corpses. It all went according to the Gray Man's plan. But you were different."

They rounded a bend in the path, and Nanami was struck in the face by a searing heat. They had arrived in the courtyard in front of the donjon. The altar in the center, which on their last visit had been buried under soot and ash, was once again in flames. And this time, the fire seemed to embody a sinister sort of power. It was surrounded by gray-faced soldiers, some fetching buckets of water, others standing in silence staring into the flames.

Taking care to avoid the sparks that were being scattered by the fire, the cat approached the main staircase into the donjon.

"What did I do that was any different?" Nanami asked. "All I did was refuse to listen to what that guy was saying to me."

"Your behavior was way beyond anything he expected. Even with guns pointing at you, you didn't give up on the books. On the contrary, you grabbed one and ran away."

"There's nothing special about that."

"And the second time you visited the castle, not only did you completely resist the power of his words, but you clearly contradicted them. The impact on him was unprecedented. His belief system was shaken to its core. In this labyrinth, the slightest waver in his convictions would shake the very foundations of his existence. That was why he became so distressed."

The cat reached the foot of the great stone staircase and turned to look at Nanami.

"And yet you even cared about him when he was suffering in pain."

It turned its head to look up to the top of the steps, then slowly began to climb, one at a time.

The towering chalk-colored walls of the castle were hazy in the cloud of smoke. The red glow of the flames was reflected in their whiteness.

"According to that man's principles, you should have taken advantage of his weakness, but you did the exact opposite. And the shock of that seems to have changed his whole way of thinking. We need to hurry."

They reached the top of the steps and slowly turned to look around them. The view was horrifying. Before them was a view of the vast layout of the castle, engulfed in flames and smoke. Nanami could no longer make out the main gate where they had come in.

From here she could see that the castle had become a huge labyrinth of turrets and spires, large and small. Smoke and flames rose from multiple locations. Burning flags and banners fluttered and danced in the sky, stirred by the currents of scorching air that blew past, carrying on them glittering sparks and the acrid smell of soot.

"The books that were removed from the donjon are still scattered about here and there within the castle walls. The Gray Man used to say that if they were contained, they would eventually lose their power, but it looks as if he decided there was no time to wait for that. And so he came to the decision to burn down the whole castle instead."

"I have to talk to him."

"You must."

The red carpet stretched out into the donjon ahead of them. It bore scorch marks in some places, probably from the sparks that blew in from the outside. The length of the corridor was littered with wads of white paper, which on closer inspection turned out to be the Prime Minister's "neo-books." It looked as if they'd been dropped and abandoned while being transported somewhere. If the fire were to reach here, it would spread immediately through the whole donjon.

The pair followed the red carpet into the General's Grand Hall. The deserted room was even more desolate than on their previous visit. The carpet was torn, cobwebs hung from the chandeliers, and the books displayed on the marble tables were covered in a thick layer of dust. It was as if decades had passed since they were last there. Perhaps being forgotten by people sped up the rate of decay more swiftly than the simple passage of time.

None of this slowed down Nanami or the cat. They rushed through the Grand Hall and on into the Prime Minister's Office, but not a soul was to be seen there, either. The bookbinding machinery that had been in such vigorous operation was a shadow of its former self. The pistons were cracked, the gears had come unstuck, and the massive press was tilting heavily to one side. Dirty bundles of paper were wedged between the parts, and at the feet of the machine lay remnants of the neo-books, now nothing but torn scraps. The image of the smiling minister sitting on his sofa in the midst of a bustling factory now felt like a dream.

Still, Nanami didn't so much as pause. She had a hunch.

Running all the way to the end of the grease-stained carpet, she found that the black sofa where the Prime Minister had once sat was gone; a brand-new door had appeared in the wall beyond. It was guarded by a single soldier.

"Who goes there?" demanded the guard. "Beyond this door lie the Chambers of His Majesty the King."

Nanami replied with all the strength she could muster.

"We have come to see the King."

The gray soldier clicked his heels and saluted.

"Visitors for His Majesty the King!" he announced. This time there was no chorus of voices echoing his words; only the guard's own voice lingering in the shadows as he stepped aside.

The double doors began to part.

On the other side was a huge space. The red carpet they'd been following became much wider and continued on deep into the room. On either side of the carpet were sturdy white marble pillars, spaced at regular intervals, which supported a high-domed ceiling. Attached to each pillar, at about the height of the average adult, was a candelabra, its lights making the crimson of the carpet all the more striking against the whiteness. By contrast, to both left and right, the room was dimly lit, and it was difficult to make out its full size, but as Nanami peered into the gloom she realized that the edges of the room were strewn with piles of discarded neo-books. The whole effect was eerie, like a bloodstained boardwalk cutting across a beach of white sand.

"Welcome to the King's Chamber," came a cold, crisp voice.

At the far end of the space, on a raised dais several steps up from floor level, was an oddly shaped white chair, apparently the King's throne. The chairback was several feet high, yet the throne was strangely simple—a plain white marble without color or adornment. On it sat a gray-suited man.

Undaunted, Nanami marched straight toward him.

The man on the throne was tall and broad-shouldered. He was neither the General nor the Prime Minister. At first glance, his strong physique made him appear youthful, but the wrinkles around his eyes and cheeks were testament to the years. The way he held himself gave him a distinctive air. Such superficial changes in appearance were of little significance. Nanami understood that now. What mattered—and was the only certainty—was that by opening each of the doors in turn she had finally arrived at this point. She didn't hesitate now as she strode right up to his throne.

"Welcome back, Nanami."

With a languid smile, the Gray King addressed her. He sat there composed and serene, and yet there was an air of decay about him. His pristine suit had scorch marks on it and was even ripped in places. His shoes were black with soot, and his deerstalker cap lay discarded at his feet. There wasn't a single guard at his side. His throne was surrounded by haphazard piles of neo-books, and the light from the candelabras sent flickering waves of light across them.

"I knew you would come," continued the King. "Even all that fire and smoke wouldn't make you run away."

He rested his elbows on the arms of his throne, and his shoulders shook with laughter. But Nanami could see a profound weariness in his gray expression.

"Well, I couldn't just let you burn everything," Nanami responded.

"Are books so important?"

"Yes, books are important. But it's not only the books. You and all those soldiers out there need to escape from here. You're in danger."

The King frowned at Nanami's pronouncement.

"Always saying things like that! You truly are the most vexing and perplexing creature," he said, his expression pained. He reached up and loosened his tie.

"I never had a single doubt until you turned up. I've always done everything in my power to help people. In fact, those who heeded my advice have ended up being very successful."

With a touch of irritation, the King tugged off his tie and tossed it aside.

"I didn't order anyone to do anything. Didn't you humans have a desire to live more freely? You were all concerned with your own gratification. You were the ones who asked for it. All I did was help to make that wish come true."

The King's voice had become a lament.

"And yet, you now claim you're concerned for my well-being?"

"I can't speak for what your experiences have been up till now," said Nanami, "but not everyone is like that. I know many people who are nothing like you describe."

"Well, although that's very sweet," replied the King, "it's just a naive fantasy on your part. If you keep that up, you'll end up as just one more person being trampled on."

He threw her a pitying look. Then he continued.

"Pursuing one's own desires, accumulating more wealth, seeking greater pleasures—this is how the current age defines freedom. It wasn't always so. There was a time when controlling your desires, freeing yourself of those desires, used to be the true definition of freedom. But that's no more than a memory now. Those days are long gone and there's no going back. My power has grown too strong to ever go back."

The King's voice reverberated through the vast space and dissipated into the darkness.

"Vulnerable people like you, Nanami, find it hard to believe, I suppose. But you'll get it. The system originally created by human desire has now escaped the grip of human beings and has started to run amok. The system has become a desire in itself and has begun to swallow up humanity."

The man's words were difficult to follow. They were already beyond Nanami's understanding.

"Hey, Your Majesty?"

It was the cat, who had finally joined the conversation.

"Why are you so desperate?"

"Desperate? Me?"

The King slowly lowered his gaze to where the cat stood by Nanami's feet.

"I see. You may be right. As a created one, who has walked alongside humans, I've observed so very much. I've seen human beings' transformation with my own eyes."

"Even if that's the case, I don't accept what you're saying," Nanami cut in. "I have a totally different perspective to yours."

The King gave a scornful laugh.

"Then why don't you show me this perspective of yours?" he remarked, glancing nonchalantly at the ceiling. "Very soon this whole place will be swallowed up by flames. What should we do? Wouldn't it be sensible to abandon the books and escape as quickly as possible? Or perhaps you plan to gather up all the books you can carry by yourself and then run? I suppose you can save some of them, although most have already been consumed by this fiery inferno. What will you do, brave girl?"

"There is a way."

As Nanami's voice cut across his, the King assumed his customary furrowed-brow expression.

"There's a way," repeated Nanami. "I can't do much by myself, but what if we all work together?"

"We all?"

The King looked at Nanami as if she were speaking a foreign language.

"You and me and all those soldiers out there. We can join forces to get the books out of the castle. That way you, me, everyone, can be rescued, along with all the books."

The King was stunned. He leaned forward, his mouth hanging open.

Nanami had never seen anyone look so shocked in her life. It wasn't only the King. The cat, too, was staring up at her, its eyes popping.

"Wh-what . . ."

The King couldn't seem to form a single clear word. His eyes darted wildly around the room.

"What are you talking about?"

"There's only so much I can do by myself. I won't leave you behind, and I won't abandon those books, either. I'm explaining to you that the best way is for us all to join forces."

After staring at Nanami for a while, his mouth still open, the King finally sat back in his throne. Then his shoulders began to tremble, ever so slightly at first, then more and more forcefully, until eventually he looked up at the ceiling and laughter exploded from him. For a while he writhed on his throne, his hand clutched to his belly as if trying to hold himself together. His laughter echoed around the great space like a chorus of voices.

"Nanami, you're quite something," he managed to squeeze out, still desperately trying to control his laughter. But he was unsuccessful, and his shoulders continued to shake as he spoke.

"I do remember after all. There used to be people like you . . . in the past."

"In the past?"

"Back then I was no more than a kind of tool. Just one way of connecting people to one another. At some point that all changed. The means became the end, trust vanished, and it was only desire that grew. So much time has passed since then . . ."

The King's eyes gazed far off into the distance.

"If only you'd come a little sooner, or . . . never mind . . ."

His voice trailed off.

At that moment, behind the King's throne, something stirred. Nanami jumped and braced herself. It was that stifling black presence.

"He's here," the cat announced, quite unnecessarily.

Within the King was now a gargantuan presence. It had been there all along—in the General's Grand Hall, and in the Prime Minister's Office too. And now the man before them in the King's Chamber had taken on the same form, and it was slowly raising its head.

"It's really been a long time," it said. The voice was entirely without feeling of any kind.

The "man" seated on the throne turned his face toward Nanami. His eyes were lifeless glass beads. Nanami felt again the sensation of a frozen hand stroking her back.

"You really are a brave girl, Nanami," said the Gray King, rising unsteadily from his throne.

That movement alone brought with it a crushing pressure that felt like a suffocating force around Nanami's throat.

"Tell me . . ." Nanami's voice was hushed. "Who are you?"

"Out of respect, I'll offer you a third hint."

Muttering cheerfully to himself, the King walked over to the one of the candelabras placed on either side of the throne. The gently flickering candles came up to about chest height.

"In any world, I am the only one who doesn't obey the laws of nature."

As Nanami watched, he picked up the candelabra and turned to look at her.

"I am the one who proliferates."

The hot candle flame licked his gray cheek, but his voice was chilling.

Then suddenly a chuckle escaped his lips.

"What if everyone had run away with the books? That's an idea I never even considered. Back then, it might have been possible, but too much time has passed."

He walked slowly back to his throne, candelabra in hand.

"Would you like to make a bet with me, Nanami?"

The question came out of nowhere.

Sensing the danger in these words, the cat stepped in front of the girl.

"Be careful, Nanami."

"I know."

The King watched their exchange with amusement.

"You really do have a strong spirit, yet you'll never be able to suppress me. After all, it's you and your kind who are driving me."

"What are you going to do?"

There was great tension in the room as the King passed by his throne and picked up the candelabra from the other side.

With the flames of the two candelabras held high, he spun around to face Nanami and the cat.

"I will become more powerful. And with that the world will become ever more prosperous. But that prosperity will be purely superficial. What I see is a bleak landscape where a handful of victors will reign over countless corpses. A world where people hurt one another, where the power of books has been completely extinguished."

"That will never happen."

Nanami felt no doubt whatsoever. She refused to acknowledge even the slightest possibility of it happening.

The King seemed satisfied with her response.

"You really believe that books have tremendous power, don't you?"

Nanami nodded emphatically. Nothing could shake her resolve. She had no reason to be afraid. Though her experiences might be far more limited than all the Gray Man had witnessed, she lived in the world. And in that world, people didn't exist alone.

"An excellent answer," said the King, grinning.

It was a terrifying expression, as if the dark and menacing presence that had been lurking within had finally shown its true face. Nanami let out a gasp and the King's voice, filled with amusement, seemed to pursue her.

"Now see if you can get out of here alive."

As he spoke, he let go of the two candelabras. They landed

with a thud on the neo-books scattered around the floor. Flames flared slightly, then immediately fire began to dance on the piles of discarded books. Within seconds, the whole area began to blaze as if a bright spotlight had been aimed at the King's feet.

Nanami stared at the King, astounded, as his wild laughter rang in her ears.

"Why?" she cried.

"Go on. Show me the power of books now!" he cried, still grinning, even as the flames began to devour his gray suit. "I think I already mentioned that this world is all about the survival of the fittest. The weak must cede to the flames of the strong. If you think you can overcome this, then please, by all means do show me that strength of yours. This is my bet with you."

From the midst of the fire, the King stretched out both arms.

"Survive! And good luck."

With one final booming laugh, he gave an elegant bow, and at once his tall figure was completely engulfed in flames. It wasn't only the King's dais that burned—the tongues of fire quickly spread throughout the whole of the chamber. The neo-books, tossed in piles on either side of the red carpet, were quickly swallowed up by orange, slithering vipers.

The cat shouted something. Nanami, glued to the spot in horror, couldn't catch its words. The fire continued to rage, now entwining the white marble pillars in its grip.

"Nanami!"

This time Nanami heard the cat's voice, but she still couldn't move. Her eyes were fixed in disbelief on the scene before her.

"We have to run! The King has taken on too much negative human emotion. There's no return from the place where he's gone."

"But..."

"There's no time to think about it!"

Nanami turned around and shuddered at what she saw.

The fire had almost reached the entrance to the King's Chamber. The path created by the red carpet barely remained. Either side of it was a sea of flames. She looked back at the dais but could no longer make out either the figure of the King or his marble throne.

"Run!"

The cat's cry spurred Nanami into action and finally she fled.

But as she flew out of the door, she pulled up short. To her horror, the Prime Minister's Office was already on fire.

Stray sparks must have ignited the machinery's oil, and the fire was spreading with alarming speed. The flames roared up between the gears. There was an odd creaking and grinding sound as the intricate machinery, unable to withstand the heat, moaned in agony.

"Hurry, Nanami!"

The cat's hoarse voice was drowned out by the unsettling noises.

To the right, the huge bookbinding machine, now engulfed

in flames, gave a loud creak. At the same time another steel tower, already leaning at a precarious angle, began to teeter.

There was no time to stop and think.

The cat lunged at Nanami and pushed her aside as the giant piece of machinery toppled to the floor with a mighty crash. The ground shook violently and there was a cloud of dust so thick that Nanami couldn't open her eyes. Then searing heat.

Nanami was thrown to the floor, and for a while she was unable to move. In the thick, billowing smoke, she clutched her left shoulder, which had slammed into the ground. She was coughing desperately but somehow managed to push herself up with one hand. Immediately she struck her head on something and looked up to see steel beams a few inches above. She gasped—if she'd been standing, there was no doubt that she'd have suffered a direct hit.

After confirming she could still move her body, she looked around at the damage, her mind still in chaos. The first thing she saw was the limp form of a tabby cat wedged into a narrow space between a steel beam and a gear wheel.

Frantically, Nanami tried to pull herself closer; it wasn't an easy task. Squeezing herself through the gaps in the broken machinery, she managed to drag herself a little way. The iron and steel were starting to heat up in the flames, but she felt neither heat nor pain.

"Hey, come on . . . open your eyes!"

She was finally able to pick up the cat, and it lay limply in her arms. It must have been struck by a piece of burning metal because there was an angry red burn mark on its side.

"Open your eyes. Please!" Nanami screamed.

"Quit panicking," replied the cat weakly, its eyes still closed.

"Are you alive?"

"It appears so. At least for now . . ."

The reply was intended to be funny but Nanami was struggling to laugh.

The cat went on, its voice shaking.

"I don't know what will happen to you if you stay here. You need to get out of here as quickly as possible."

"I would never leave you behind."

"It's going to be very difficult to run with a cat in your arms."

The cat cracked open one green eye and peered around. All it could see were countless bits of machinery. There wasn't even space to stand up, and there were very few unobstructed spaces between the tangled piles of cogwheels, gears, and beams. Here and there the equipment was still burning; the air was filled with thick black smoke.

"Quickly, just go!" the cat urged her.

"I'm not leaving you."

"I'm glad to hear you say it, although if those words come from despair, then I have no use for them."

"But look at you!"

"I can handle this," said the cat, with a weak smile.

It was the same line that Nanami herself always used. She attempted to force a smile in return, but couldn't manage it.

"How can you say that when you have absolutely no idea what to do next?"

"You have no evidence of that," the cat announced, without conviction. "Hope makes a show of reviving—not with any reason to back it."

Nanami's eyes became big.

"Well, isn't that the nature of hope?" said the cat with a tiny laugh. Then it passed out again, its body going limp.

Nanami decided to save her strength, and instead of trying to revive the cat, this time she checked that it was still breathing, then hugged her feline friend close to her chest. After a desperate look around for someone who might help—of course there was no one—she realized she didn't even know which direction the exit was. All she could see was metal, smoke, and flames.

Her head was growing hotter from the fire, and her eyes stung from the smoke. When she tried to wipe them, the back of her hand came away smeared with something black. She realized her face must be covered in soot.

Clinging on somehow to the cat, Nanami began to crawl under the steel frame of the broken machinery, but she soon found her way blocked. If she went any farther, she would be right in the fire.

"Hope makes a show of reviving."

Nanami muttered the words to herself, clutching at the last slivers of hope in her heart, hugging them close along with the cat as she searched for a way through.

"Hope makes a show of reviving," she repeated, her voice turning hoarse, as she desperately searched for any kind of way forward.

Every time she hit a dead end, she turned to look for another exit. And each time that she was forced to change direction, the hope that had begun to glimmer in her heart faded once again. A heavy, chilling despair began to creep up on her.

"Hope makes a show of reviving..."

Nanami wondered how long it had been there—the brightly colored creature that fluttered in the corner of her vision. It was a beautiful butterfly, in glorious red, blue, and yellow hues. Amid the heat and thick smoke, this rainbow-colored jewel danced in the air.

Nanami didn't question why it was there, nor did she believe it was a hallucination. Looking at it somehow made her feel calmer and, despite the discouragement in her heart, she was able to keep going.

Chasing the butterfly, she crawled under the steel frame and squeezed her body between broken beams, and dodging the flames, she searched for a way out. She didn't stop for a moment, even after the glittering butterfly vanished from sight.

Suddenly, from somewhere and nowhere, there was a deep rumbling sound. The castle had started to crumble. Fighting the fear that the exits might be blocked, Nanami kept moving, but she found no room to pass between all the gears and cogwheels that were piled up on the floor.

There's no way out...

Nanami bit her lip and hugged the cat closer to her chest. As she fought to control the tears that threatened to overflow from her eyes, a tiny black shadow came rushing toward her. Deftly maneuvering between iron, steel, and flame, it ran right up to Nanami and came to a halt in front of her. This time it wasn't a butterfly; it was a little mouse.

Nanami gasped, not because she was startled by the mouse, but because she recognized it: a field mouse with greenish fur and a sleepy-looking face.

The mouse stared back at Nanami as if waiting for her to call its name. A warm feeling began to spread in the girl's chest.

"Y—You're . . ."

The mouse smiled.

"Aren't you that mouse poet?"

The mouse stood up. Shyly, it put a hand to its chest and bowed politely—a gesture that Nanami had seen many times. Then, its left hand still resting on its chest, the mouse nodded toward its right.

"That way?"

The mouse nodded again.

"There's a way out over there?"

Even before Nanami had finished her question, the mouse scurried away, darting between bits of machinery, and was quickly out of sight. Nanami hurried after it, still cradling the cat.

This way, there didn't seem to be any fire, and Nanami found a gap to crawl through. Squeezing her way through crumbling debris, and clinging to hope that could also crumble at any moment, she managed to continue. Then, to her surprise, she found herself in a space tall enough to stand.

She'd escaped from the labyrinth of steel. Around her was

a scene of devastation with toppled pillars and white marble reduced to rubble; at least the fire hadn't reached this place yet. For a moment she didn't recognize her surroundings, but then she saw a shattered chandelier at her feet.

"It's the General's Grand Hall."

As if in response, pinpoints of light appeared that seemed to mark the way through the debris before her. Like beacons guiding a ship, all the books in the room had begun to glow softly. On one of the toppled marble tables, Nanami saw *Twenty Thousand Leagues Under the Sea*. *Treasure Island* was partially buried by bricks. A little farther away lay *Moby-Dick*, its cover practically torn to shreds.

Nanami stood and with her eyes traced the trail of lights. At the end she could make out the grand doorway, partially destroyed. There appeared to be just enough space left for a small girl carrying a cat to squeeze her way through.

Adjusting her grip on the cat, Nanami picked her way through the rubble, dodging shards of chandelier and kicking bricks out of her path. Just as she was about to pass through the remains of the doorway, she stopped and turned back toward the General's Grand Hall and the glowing books that had lit her way.

"Thank you," she whispered, as she slipped out through the door.

Beyond was the relative safety of the wide, red-carpeted corridor, but there was no time to linger. Gray-faced soldiers were gathering at the entrance to the donjon, arriving not only from the main stairway, but also appearing from behind pillars and the small staircases in adjoining corridors. Even as the fire already threatened to engulf the outer walls of the castle and the courtyard, they paid no attention at all, continuing to bustle around the interior of the donjon.

When one of them spotted Nanami standing amid the rubble, he gave a cry of alarm and raised his musket. As Nanami leapt behind one of the piles, she heard a sharp burst of gunfire, a volley of shots ricocheting off the bricks and sending chunks of stone flying in all directions.

"They're hiding."

"The King's orders are to capture them."

Empty voices devoid of emotion echoed off the walls and high ceiling, and seemed to come at Nanami from every direction.

She couldn't move. All she could do was huddle behind the heaps of debris and clasp the cat close to her chest. There were too many of them, and they had guns. Nothing could be gained from rushing out from her hiding place.

"Hope makes a show of reviving, hope makes a show of reviving . . ." Nanami repeated the words as if in prayer.

She heard the soldiers' footsteps approaching, their orderly rhythm reminiscent of the bookbinding machine that had churned out the neo-books. They marched on, closer and closer.

"Hope makes a show of reviving . . ."

Seeking some sort of salvation, Nanami stared up at the ceiling. Her voice froze in midchant as a gray face intruded on the periphery of her vision.

"Found them!" The gray soldier's gray voice rang in her ears.

With machinelike precision, he aimed his musket at Nanami. Was it her imagination, or was the movement unnaturally slow? She closed her eyes tightly, still clinging to the cat.

A high-pitched sound tore the air apart. Not just a single shot, but multiple gunshots ringing out one after the other, followed a moment later by a heavy thud.

Nanami cracked open one eye and was amazed at what she saw. Lying on the ground before her was the gray-faced soldier. And in his place stood a tall man brandishing a long sword. As she stared in amazement, the man placed his sword into the scabbard at his waist, dropped gracefully to one knee, and flashed her a bright smile.

"Is all well, my dear?"

As he spoke, several more men came rushing over and formed a protective circle around Nanami. These were no gray soldiers. Each man was dressed in a vivid shade of blue, with a sword at his side and a musket in his right hand. On the chest of each bright blue uniform was a beautifully embroidered white cross.

Nanami immediately recognized the design. It had to be impossible, but she was sure she knew that emblem.

"Musketeers!" she said aloud, to which the man smiled and bowed his head.

Although armed with a sword and a musket, there was nothing coarse or brutal about the man; his movements were refined and his smile elegant.

"We got here in time. That's the important thing."

As he spoke, his sharp eye was caught by movement at the

entrance to the donjon. Beyond the end of the red carpet a new band of gray soldiers had appeared.

"Porthos!" he cried.

The giant of a man standing behind him responded. "Understood. Musketeers, prepare!"

At the giant's booming command, the musketeers quickly formed two rows and lifted their weapons. Porthos raised a hefty arm, then, as he brought it down, a dozen or so muskets were fired in unison, cutting down the band of gray soldiers that had just arrived.

"You're not injured are you, Nanami?" asked the tall musketeer, paying no attention to the battle taking place behind him. "I apologize for the delay, but it seems we arrived in the nick of time."

"You know my name?"

"Of course we do. We came to rescue you."

"To rescue me?"

There was a sharp whistling sound, and a bullet grazed the man's cheek. He turned to watch the battle, and Nanami saw one of his band of musketeers fall silently to the ground, shot.

More grey soldiers were appearing at the donjon entrance. The musketeers were taking cover behind fallen columns and other rubble. They were severely outnumbered.

"Porthos, can't you do something?"

"What are you talking about? There are far too many of them."

The hulking musketeer came over and crouched next to Nanami, clicking his tongue as he swiftly reloaded his musket.

"So many of them, and they just keep advancing. It's as if they want to be targets."

"Quit your grumbling, Porthos. We just need to hold out a little longer."

"I know, but we can't go on like this much more. What's taking Athos so long to get here?"

As the giant Porthos fired his musket between the piles of rubble, another musketeer was struck. Nanami was frozen, unable to move or speak.

Despite the dire situation, the tall musketeer didn't lose his serene smile. *This must be Aramis*, Nanami thought.

"As he has just explained to us, Nanami," he said, "even the valiant Porthos here can't hold off the enemy forever. Our position is untenable."

He pointed a long index finger at one of the corridors branching off to the left. Beyond a column, there was a tiny spiral staircase.

"Please go that way. We'll hold them off here."

Nanami shook her head.

"I can't abandon you after you came here to rescue me."

"Noble sentiments," declared the tall musketeer, with a playful grin. "It's gratifying to know our efforts weren't in vain. Don't worry about us. As long as you are safe, we can't be brought down."

"As long as I'm safe?"

"You are the King's target. And to protect you is our challenge. We will accept that challenge, shred it into pieces, and send it back. That's the way of the musketeers."

The tall musketeer was unperturbed, standing there amid a hail of bullets. It was not that the danger had passed, just that he didn't know how to give in to it.

"But . . ." Nanami searched for the right words. "You came here to rescue me, and I am the only one running away."

"You're not running away," the giant Porthos cut in. Beneath his thick mustache there was a defiant smile. "This slip of a man is correct. You have to escape this castle. And that is why we are here."

"Enough with the 'slip of a man' business. You may just refer to me as a gentleman."

The giant man snorted at the look of displeasure on his comrade's face.

"Call yourself a gentleman? You're nothing but an indiscriminate womanizer."

"You've got some nerve, Porthos! Just you wait until this battle's done, then I'm going to make a point of shooting you in the head."

"If you have such bullets to spare, then hand them over because I'm running out."

Throughout the sharp-tongued banter, they continued to load and fire their muskets, their movements measured and precise.

There was nothing Nanami could say. It was hard to be sure exactly what was happening, but she knew that some great power was doing all in its might to protect her. She struggled to hold back the tears, knowing this was not the time or place to cry. Instead, she hugged the cat and bowed deeply to the two musketeers.

The tall musketeer smiled back at her, but the giant behind him dropped his musket and drew his sword from his scabbard. The other musketeers all followed suit, until everyone was standing with swords drawn. Nanami looked around to see gentle reassuring smiles from every one of them.

"Go on, Nanami," said the tall musketeer, giving her a gentle nudge.

As Nanami leapt out from behind the rubble, the musketeers also emerged from the shadows to cover her back. As she sprinted to her left, the sound of gunfire behind her changed to that of a fierce swordfight. Out of the corner of her eye she saw someone fall but didn't stop to look back.

She rushed down the side corridor and sprang onto the spiral staircase. There was no hesitation in her movements because she had immediately recognized it as the same one she had climbed the first time she'd been in the castle. Although the size and scale of the castle had changed, her memory of the event remained clear. She reflected how, then, the cat had been running ahead of her but was now curled up in her arms.

"Hope makes a show of reviving..."

Nanami chanted the words like a magic spell as she put all her strength into climbing.

For a brief moment, there was a wheezing sound from deep in her throat and she felt a chill travel down the back of her neck.

She'd been running at full speed, weaving around steel beams and leaping over rubble, dodging flying bullets. How could her body survive this unscathed? If she had an asthma attack now, she wouldn't be able to run anymore.

"Hope makes a show of reviving."

Now Nanami heard footsteps below her—intimidating, authoritative, marching in an orderly fashion up the stairs. She knew it wasn't the musketeers, and she couldn't tell at that moment if what she was feeling was fear, sadness, or pain.

The worrying sounds in her chest and throat began to spread. It was difficult to catch her breath, and her breathing became erratic. Her legs were getting heavier as she continued to climb.

"Hope makes a show of reviving."

Nanami's feet came to a stop. Still she hadn't given up. With one hand supporting the cat, she used the other to reach for her inhaler. But, as she brought it to her mouth, it slipped from her shaky grasp and rolled down the stone steps with a clatter.

She froze in horror as her throat constricted.

"Hope makes . . ."

She couldn't continue.

All her strength drained from her body.

"Don't give up!"

The voice came from ahead of her.

She looked up and was shocked by what she saw. A gray-faced soldier was standing a few steps above her.

A featureless face with a gray complexion and expressionless glassy eyes. Despite the familiar eerie appearance, Nanami felt her intuition kick in. There was something different about this soldier.

His bloodless lips moved.

"You can't give up so soon," he said and, without changing his expression, extended a hand. As if drawn by some unseen force, Nanami reached out her own hand and grasped the soldier's, feeling herself pulled upward with great strength. The soldier continued to pull her along, all the while speaking to her in a monotone.

"Here it is the power of the heart that is the strongest. It's not running at full speed that triggers an asthma attack. It's anxiety and despair."

Even before he finished speaking, Nanami felt scorching air and smoke on her face. They'd reached the top of the castle walls. Sparks of fire swirled around them.

Nanami gazed down to see masses of soldiers gathering below like a swarm of ants. She guessed they were under the King's orders—they made no move to try to avoid the fire. Their only purpose was to pursue Nanami. The steps at the entrance of the castle were also teeming with soldiers.

"What about the musketeers?" she said.

"Don't worry about them. They're holding their own down there," said the gray soldier, his voice calm and reassuring. "More importantly, will you be able to run again?"

The man asking her this question was to all intents and purposes the same as all the gray soldiers down below, which was extremely confusing to Nanami.

"I think you already know where the exit is," the soldier continued.

Nanami quickly looked around the castle walls. Flames were now licking the battlements at the top, staining the whole view bright red. But in between the flames she caught a glimpse of a small turret. It was the same turret she had dived into with the cat the first time they'd come.

"That tower . . ."

"That's it. Through the door in that turret. There's a passageway."

"It's on fire!"

The conversation was brought to an abrupt end by the emergence of a band of gray soldiers from the spiral staircase. Nanami's ally spun around to position himself at the top of the staircase, simultaneously striking the lead soldier with his elbow. It was a brilliant move, causing the soldier to topple backward, taking with him the dozen or so soldiers standing immediately below. They yelled as they tumbled together to the bottom of the staircase.

The soldier spoke once more in his calm voice.

"That will buy you some time. All that remains is for you to run through the fire and smoke."

The man's voice was not only calm, it was filled with vitality. It didn't match the gray, featureless face before her.

"And what about you?" Nanami asked him.

"If I go with you, there will be no one left here to hold them off. I can manage to keep them within this narrow staircase for a while."

"But I can't leave you behind. I don't want anyone else to get hurt."

The soldier looked surprised.

"Everyone is fighting for my sake," Nanami continued. "I can't just—"

"You are a kind soul, Nanami. But you really have to escape from here."

"You know me too? Who are you? I want you to come with me."

Nanami was shouting now, yet the voice that responded was as gentle and calm as ever.

"It's okay. I'm not going to succumb. The musketeers will be fine too—and that stubborn cat. As long as we deliver you safely from this place, none of us will perish."

The mysterious soldier patted Nanami's soot-and-grime-streaked hair as he spoke.

"What a terrible King to put a lovely young lady like you through such an awful ordeal."

"You know what . . ."

Nanami suddenly raised her voice.

"I know you!"

She was interrupted by a volley of gunshots coming from far below the castle wall. The soldier hastily put an arm around Nanami and pulled her down to safety. As the gunfire continued, Nanami knelt on the stone walkway and stared into the gray face. The words bubbling up in her mind were so dazzling she could barely speak them. And so, as if gently scooping up a very precious object, she whispered them to him.

"You really are a master of disguise."

The soldier raised an eyebrow and looked at her.

"A gentleman thief who sneaks in anywhere he likes to help a person in need," she continued.

The gray-faced soldier shrugged slightly, then chuckled. The lifeless mask transformed instantly to a playful grin.

"I have been defeated," he announced. "You are quite the detective, Nanami."

Another band of gray soldiers emerged from the stairwell. The gentleman thief neatly dodged a bayonet thrust, then grabbed the gun, twisting it out of his opponent's hands and dealing him a hard blow in the chest with the butt of the weapon. As before, the soldiers following screamed as they tumbled back down the stairwell.

"There's no end to them," he muttered, brushing the soot from his shoulders. Then he peered over the edge of the battlements.

"Well, it seems the main force has finally arrived."

He tossed the stolen musket over the wall and urged Nanami to look down below.

A large group of gray soldiers were gathered in the central courtyard, but a band of men on horseback had burst in from outside the castle walls. They poured into the courtyard in a coordinated line, and on the signal of a single gunshot all drew their swords and fell upon the gray soldiers, who were thrown into panic and chaos.

Nanami spotted the cavalry's flag, fluttering resplendently. It was an ornate white cross on a blue background.

"That's the . . ." Her voice trailed off.

It was a beautiful flag she had seen many times in books. Not only beautiful but shining with pride and courage.

The gentleman thief shielded his eyes with one hand and smiled in delight.

"Finally, all the musketeers are here. It seems you're a popular girl, Nanami. That's quite a number."

Nanami followed the direction in which the thief was looking and saw a whole stream of white crosses on blue pouring in through the castle gates. Though not a massive army, these were elite, select soldiers, and under their attack the gray soldiers quickly began to fall.

But due to their sheer numbers, the gray army didn't collapse completely. As individuals fell, more men would emerge from various parts of the castle, advancing into battle like a machine. Fighting broke out everywhere.

"Right, then," said the gentleman thief, placing a hand on Nanami's shoulder. "Now the rest is up to you. The enemy is going to keep on coming, but the musketeers can't keep fighting forever."

"But I have to leave them all here?"

He shook his head.

"That's not what you're doing. You're clearing a path for everyone."

Nanami barely even noticed the bullet that whizzed by, almost grazing her ear. She knew what she had to do. She knew, yet her legs wouldn't move. She couldn't stem the emotion that was overflowing, neither could she find any words.

When she eventually opened her mouth to speak, the gentleman thief raised a finger to stop her.

"We don't need any thanks from you. In fact, quite the reverse."

Nanami closed her mouth again then turned to face the fiery wall. She observed the battlements engulfed in flames, the snaking columns of black smoke, the crumbling walkway, and beyond it all, her goal, the turret that concealed the escape route.

It would have been a lie to say she wasn't terrified, but her feet didn't falter. She hadn't come this far alone.

From behind her, once again she heard those eerie mechanical footsteps on the stairs.

"Go, Nanami!" the powerful voice of Lupin the thief rang out. "Run with all your might!"

Keeping the cat close, Nanami leapt into the fire.

At some point the rain had stopped. The moon shone through gaps in the cloud, casting a pattern of shadows and light on the portico in front of the library. There was no wind to ripple the puddles on the street, and they shimmered golden in the moonlight. Next to the flower beds were a myriad of tiny puddles, each reflecting the light as if some eccentric millionaire had run around scattering gold coins on the ground.

Seiichiro's car was still parked in the same place, but it

was enveloped in silence and moonlight, and Nanami had the impression she was returning to a different world from the one she had left.

Both hands hugging her precious bundle, Nanami turned to look back, catching the moment when the bluish-white path she had just taken vanished like morning dew in sunlight. All that remained was the totally unremarkable glass entryway to the library.

"Nanami!"

Hearing her father call out, she turned back to the car.

Nanami had no sense of how much time had passed. It could have been ages or just moments, but her father was standing in the exact same spot by the car as when she'd set out.

"Nanami, are you all right?" he asked as he came running toward her. "Are you hurt? How's your asthma?"

Amid the rapid-fire questions, Seiichiro gave his daughter a big bear hug.

In fact, Nanami felt perfectly fine. Despite running through a blazing inferno, nothing at all seemed to have been affected—not her body or even her clothes. The only change was her priceless cargo.

"Dad?"

Nanami stretched out her arms to show him what she was holding. Seiichiro's eyes widened in surprise.

It was a book.

An ancient picture book.

The book wasn't just old—it was covered in scorch marks, blackened with soot, and torn around the edges. Even so the illustration on the cover was clearly visible. A cat with jade-green eyes looked back at them, an imperious expression on its face.

"What's this book?"

"I just found it in my arms."

"But this is . . ."

Nanami's father looked pleasantly surprised.

"Don't you remember? I bought you this picture book a long time ago. You loved it so much . . . I thought it was lost forever."

"I do remember. I remember turning these pages so many times."

Seiichiro didn't move for a while, his eyes never leaving the book. Eventually he put one hand on his daughter's shoulder and looked her in the eyes, deadly serious.

"Can you tell me what happened?"

"Even if I did, I doubt you'd believe it."

"Well, that's probably true."

Nanami was surprised by the answer. There was a smile on Seiichiro's face.

"Tell me anyway. I'd really like to know where you found your precious picture book. Did you take a voyage to the bottom of the ocean, or the dark side of the moon? Or perhaps you journeyed to Sirius, light-years away from here? I promise I'll listen to whatever story you want to tell me, on the condition that you tell it to me properly."

Her father's relaxed smile and gentle voice brought back a surge of memories for Nanami. When they used to go to the library together, this same smile had been on the face of the man watching over her. With that same rich voice, he would talk endlessly of Captain Nemo's adventures or the exploits of the Count of Monte Cristo. Nanami could even see the sunshine streaming in as they sat in that familiar window seat.

Tears welled up in Nanami's eyes. This time it was impossible to hold them back and they flowed freely down her cheeks.

"Hey, hey, don't cry out here," her father teased.

He turned to look at the shimmering rain puddles and scratched his head as if embarrassed.

"You're going to make your dad cry too."

THE ONE WHO QUESTIONS

The first snowfall of the year had come, slightly later than usual, and the town was dusted with a thin layer of white powder.

It was mid-December, and there was an air of festivity, with more people out on the streets than usual. Down the side alleys, young kids were running about in excitement. There wasn't enough snow for a snowball fight, but it was still fun to play in.

"It's kind of bright outside, isn't it?"

At Nanami's words, Rintaro looked up from the cash register.

"It's odd," he said, tapping at the keys. "When you think

of snow you imagine something harsh and cold; in fact it's strangely bright and sometimes even has some warmth about it."

A customer had just left after buying a couple of books. He was an elderly gentleman, apparently a distinguished scholar, who had purchased a thin, ancient-looking book with the single word *Analects* on the cover, and another heavier tome titled *The Golden Bough* that came in a box with gold leaf decoration. Nanami had been fascinated.

"Want a cup of tea?"

Nanami nodded and Rintaro placed the kettle on the little paraffin heater. Nanami sat next to it and waited for the water to boil.

Inside the bookshop, the only sounds were the crackling of the heater and the occasional whooping of children running by in the street.

"Is your father coming to pick you up again this evening?" Rintaro asked as he got the cups out of the cupboard behind him. Nanami shook her head.

"I'm going to take the train this time. I have a book to return to the library on the way."

"Will you be okay?"

"You know, I'm already in junior high school and I thought it was about time I was able to ride a train by myself. I told my father and he said that I could. And that if I had any problems, I should ask the people around me for help."

"I see."

Rintaro arranged the cups on the desk.

"I wonder if your father understands."

"Yes, not everything . . . But it turned out that he got more of it than I thought he would," she said, laughing.

———

That night, after getting back from the library, Nanami had placed her cherished picture book on the study bookshelf, then told her father as much of the story as she could. Naturally, she made sure to omit the most frightening parts and reframed it as the innocent adventures of a child, which was something she was rather good at doing.

A whole range of expressions passed across Seiichiro's face—disbelief, shock, anger—and by the end, he was left with a look of utter bewilderment.

"This is way too difficult for me to handle," he said with a sigh as he massaged his temples. "If your mother had been here, we could have asked her what she thought."

He smiled wryly, and Nanami read a mix of loneliness, sentiment, and humor on her father's face.

Instead of grilling his daughter for further details, Seiichiro devoted time to making promises. He made Nanami promise that she would always consult him when in trouble and not engage in dangerous activities alone. In return, he promised to reduce his work hours and spend more time at home. This didn't mean that work would be easy, but . . .

"I may have had my priorities a bit wrong."

Nanami silently listened as, constructively and patiently, he wove his words with great thoughtfulness.

At the end of their conversation, Seiichiro grinned at his daughter.

"Shall I take you to that Natsuki bookshop from time to time?"

The suggestion was totally unexpected. Nanami, overwhelmed with joy, jumped up suddenly, banging her knee on the desk in her excitement.

She had already returned all the volumes of the Lupin collection to the library. According to Mr. Hamura, after a thorough check of the shelves, it appeared that no books were missing.

"Well, this is a library, after all. Books come and go."

Whether it was a sarcastic comment or just Old Ham muttering to himself, Nanami had no trouble letting his words wash over her.

Things had begun ever so slightly to change and, for the most part, to move forward.

"Here you are."

Rintaro brought her a freshly poured cup of tea.

The flame of the paraffin heater reflected in the beautiful porcelain teacup. As she picked it up, Nanami's mind was filled with a series of random thoughts: a massive castle, flickering flames, fallen machinery, and beyond that, the figure of a lone man.

"Are you thinking about it again?" Rintaro asked her.

"I can't help but wonder about everything that happened. It was so frightening, yet it feels like I discovered something very important."

As he lifted his own teacup, Rintaro gently interrupted.

"You don't have to rush to put it into words. You won the bet against the King. Maybe that's all that matters for now. You made it back. That's probably why all the missing books were returned."

"Yes, but . . ." Nanami continued to gaze at the ripples on the surface of her tea. "'The one who proliferates' . . . It's such a strange phrase. And creepy too."

Behind his glasses, Rintaro frowned slightly.

"'The only one who doesn't obey the laws of nature,'" he mused. "That's what the Gray King said."

"Do you have any idea what he meant?"

"Not exactly . . . I do have my suspicions."

After a slight pause, Rintaro continued, choosing his words with care.

"Everything in the world inevitably decays over time. Iron rusts, apples rot, and living beings age. Without intervention, even the strongest walls will crumble, and the power of human emotions cannot resist the flow of time. Anger, inspiration, and even sadness will eventually be swept away by the waves of oblivion."

"So, that's the law of nature?"

"Of course, the way things appear can change depending on your perspective. But it is a fundamental principle that things decay over time. However, among the things created by humankind, some never decay. In fact, on the contrary, there are things that, over time, steadily and slowly gain strength. Things that, just by existing, continue to grow and multiply—or, in other words, proliferate."

Suddenly, a vision of a massive wall came to Nanami's mind. The castle that grew larger each time she visited.

"If the Gray King is what I imagine then, Nanami, you have been facing something tremendous. An entity that steadily grows and multiplies, continuing to cause ever more distortions, even now."

"Does such a thing exist?"

"It does."

Rintaro responded quietly but clearly. And with his brief reply, Nanami felt the temperature in the shop suddenly drop.

"You mean—"

"We mustn't rush to conclusions."

Rintaro was as cautious as ever.

"There's no evidence that what I'm imagining is correct. There's so much I don't understand. The theory that something increases just by existing is inherently flawed. And the distortions that result . . . what compensates for those . . . ? Well, I'm not even sure there's any compensation at all . . ."

Rintaro's voice had dropped to a murmur, as if he were organizing his own thoughts rather than speaking to Nanami.

Nanami waited patiently as he sat by the flickering heater, lost in thought.

He didn't have a clear answer for her. Rintaro was always careful, thoughtful, and never rushed to conclusions. He wasn't in the habit of spouting platitudes to settle matters quickly. Nanami found this reassuring.

She recalled something the cat had once said to her.

Words are like a telescope. They help you see the things you want to see, but they leave you blind to everything else.

She believed that was true. If you rushed to put everything into words, you were bound to miss many things. The world was too complicated to be completely replaced by words.

"What? You've got a visitor again? That's unusual."

Nanami looked up in surprise at the sound of a lively female voice. A tall, slender woman with a pixie haircut was peeking out from the staircase behind the cash register. "This is my wife, Sayo," Rintaro explained to the bewildered Nanami. "This must be the first time you've met?"

"Your wife?" Nanami repeated, stunned.

"I've been in Europe for the past month doing translation work," Sayo explained. "I just got back yesterday."

"Rintaro, you're married?"

In hindsight it was rather a rude question, but at that moment Nanami was too flustered to think. She was quite shocked by her own loud voice and quickly shut up.

"You wouldn't think so, would you?" said Sayo with a

chuckle. "Most people wouldn't expect the introverted owner of a used bookshop like this one to have a wife."

"No, no, not at all," Nanami protested, as Sayo stepped out into the aisle.

"I'm Sayo Natsuki. You must be Nanami. It's nice to meet you. Rintaro has told me all about you."

Nanami hastily shook the graceful hand that Sayo extended to her.

"I'm Nanami Kosaki."

"Just call me Sayo," she responded casually, reaching for Rintaro's cup on the cashier's desk. She briefly touched her lips to the hot liquid before pulling away with a start, though even that motion seemed graceful to Nanami. Rintaro gave Sayo a reproachful yet tender look. Unperturbed, Sayo returned the cup and regarded Nanami.

"First things first, welcome. But there's one important thing you should know . . ."

Nanami looked worried.

"You can ask Rintaro's advice about anything, but don't overdo it. He's reliable, but he tends to overthink things. If you spend too much time together, you might end up getting lost in his mental labyrinth," Sayo explained.

She crouched down in front of the younger girl so that she was just below her eye level. "I've heard the whole story. You went to a terrible place and you made it back safely. That's the important thing. Other than that, time will tell."

"Time?" Nanami asked.

"Exactly. Time is crucial. Like tea—it doesn't taste good

once it's gone cold, but if you're in too much of a hurry to take a sip, you'll get burned. The important thing is to relax and browse the bookshelves until the temperature is right."

The grin on Sayo's face was infectious, and Nanami found herself laughing out loud.

There was no affectation or counterfeit in Sayo's voice, and Nanami could feel her genuine concern. She was the kind of person who was able to express her feelings with authenticity.

Nanami could clearly picture the relationship between Rintaro and Sayo. The cerebral, deeply thoughtful Rintaro and the more cheerful Sayo would run this tiny bookshop together very effectively by balancing each other out.

"Since you're here, you should ask Rintaro for some book recommendations and borrow a few from the shelves. Just be careful, though, because sometimes he recommends some really heavy stuff," Sayo said, ignoring Rintaro's protestations.

Nanami felt drawn to the older woman's warmth.

"Sayo-san, have you also met the mysterious cat?" she asked.

Nanami didn't understand why the question popped into her head, but she had a feeling that Sayo must have done.

The older woman's smile was extra bright.

"Of course. Such an arrogant, yet wise and charming creature."

"Do you think I'll ever get to meet it again?"

Nanami, still clutching her teacup, leaned forward.

"I dragged that cat all over with me, caused it all kinds of trouble, but I never got to say thank you properly, or goodbye."

Sayo didn't answer, instead turning to look at Rintaro who had started to laugh.

"What are you laughing for?" she asked him.

"Sorry," Rintaro said hastily, waving his hand in apology at his wife's irritated expression. "It's just that I once asked the cat the exact same question: if we'd ever meet again."

"And what did it say?"

"I clearly remember. It said that it was a cliché."

Nanami's eyes grew round.

"I was asking a serious question, but that cat just sneered at me. Such a mean creature."

But Rintaro's eyes betrayed that he was enjoying the reminiscences.

An image of the cat's face flashed through Nanami's mind, with its gentle expression of nostalgia when it talked about its past adventures with a certain boy. Rintaro's expression now was strikingly similar.

"Maybe the cat won't come back. That's okay. Just because it has stopped showing up doesn't mean it's gone completely. It just achieved its goal," Rintaro explained.

"Its goal?"

"I don't really know the truth. That difficult cat never explained anything properly. It was never really cute enough to be a cat and was a terrible guide in those labyrinths."

Rintaro paused a moment.

"Anyway," he continued, "there's no need to worry. If there was something you wanted to say to it, I'm sure it's already got the message."

Nanami nodded and didn't ask any further questions. These were people who obviously knew a lot more than she did.

"The important thing is to cherish whatever is in front of you," Sayo spoke up.

"Everything?" Nanami asked.

"Yes. People and objects, of course, but not only that. All kinds of things. Words, time, more abstract things . . . Everything has a soul. The things you cherish all have a soul and will always protect you. Just the way that cat came to you."

Rintaro took up the conversation.

"That's why we have to be careful. Something that has been in the hands of a twisted soul will also acquire a twisted soul. It's sad but I'm convinced it's true."

Nanami nodded once again.

"I'll remember that," she said.

Sayo smiled in response.

Nanami lightly sipped from her teacup. The pleasant aroma of Earl Grey wafted into the air.

―――

Fine, powdery snowflakes kept falling well into the evening. Nothing that could be described as a heavy snowfall, but it stuck enough to drape the pavements in a light cover of white.

When Rintaro offered to take her home, Nanami shook her head and simply thanked him. She was determined to increase the number of things she could do by herself.

Walk to the station, take the train, and get off at the nearest station to the library to return a book. All this while snow was falling. For most people, this would be no more than an ordinary day; for Nanami, it was a small adventure.

She felt fine both physically and mentally. And her inhaler was safely in her pocket. She also had a new emergency inhaler to replace the one that she had dropped inside the labyrinth. She was fully prepared for her little trip.

Nanami opened up her umbrella under the dancing snowflakes and set out slowly. At the station, she was careful to rest partway up the stairs. She was very surprised to find how crowded the train was, and she had managed to stand all the way to her stop. The library wasn't too far from the station—just a short walk through a residential area. She reached it without any problems.

All that was left was for her to return the book to the counter but, feeling a little tired from her journey, she decided to head up to the second floor and take a break in her usual seat by the window. Back in that gray castle she had had much more energy; it turned out that reality and the labyrinth were rather different.

The second floor of the library was as quiet as ever; there was not a soul to be seen. Rather than being a result of the bad weather, it was more just the way the library always was in the evenings. The elderly woman she occasionally saw was absent today.

Looking out of the window, Nanami noticed that the black roofs of the residential area were gradually turning white, making the outdoors seem brighter than usual, even though it was already five o'clock in the evening. Some children had gathered in the adjacent elementary school's playground and were happily playing in the snow. If it kept snowing this heavily overnight, tomorrow they might be able to build snowmen.

Doesn't look like it'll stop anytime soon, Nanami thought as she rested her elbows on the desk and gazed up at the thick snow clouds.

She wandered awhile along the aisles. She could see nothing particularly unusual going on. The shelves with their gaps like missing teeth were mostly filled now. Of course, there were still some empty spaces but, as Old Ham had rightly pointed out, it was the nature of library books to come and go.

"I wonder if everything is back to normal now . . ."

Nanami spoke the words aloud as a kind of incantation to help her resolve some lingering concerns in her mind.

Sayo was right; you might think about many topics without finding any answers. To enjoy the perfect cup of tea, it was important to wait for it to reach the right temperature.

"When should I head back . . . ?" she mused quietly. If only the snow would stop, it would be easier to get home, but it looked as if it would continue for the rest of the day. If conditions worsened much further, even walking could become difficult.

As she pondered her options, Nanami glanced around her. Her eyes stopped as she spotted a lone figure in what she had believed to be a deserted space. A tall man was standing in front of the vending machine by the lifts. The metallic clink of coins being inserted into the machine made a tinny high-pitched noise that rang out across the floor. Then came the heavy sound of a plastic bottle dropping into the retrieval slot.

For some reason, Nanami found herself fixated on his movements. She watched him use his left hand to pick up the bottle and his right to retrieve his change, before making his way along the aisle between the bookshelves and the reading corner.

Then it struck her . . . the man was wearing a gray suit and matching deerstalker cap.

Utterly composed, he strolled past the bookshelves. Literature, philosophy, history . . . he passed each in turn, finally arriving at the section marked "Economics." There he turned and started toward the reading corner where Nanami was sitting.

Unflinching, Nanami watched the man in the suit walk straight toward her. He arrived at the table, set down his bottle of tea, then took the cap from his head.

"Is this seat taken?" he asked.

His face was gray, that familiar expressionless face devoid of joy, anger, or pain. Frozen.

Nanami clasped her hands together over her book, then slowly raised just her right hand to gesture to the chair opposite.

―

The Gray King pulled out the chair at an angle, sat down, and leisurely crossed his legs. After carefully lining up the coins from his right hand on the table, he pushed the bottle of tea toward Nanami. She didn't react.

He turned his emotionless gaze on her.

"I thought you liked tea."

"It depends on the circumstances."

"I see," said the King, unperturbed, toying with the coins on the table.

"Why are you here?" Nanami asked curtly. Her voice didn't tremble. She was on her guard but had surprised even herself at how quickly she had regained her composure.

Each time she had faced the Gray Man until now, it had been inside the gray castle. Whether it was in the General's Grand Hall, the Prime Minister's Office, or the King's Chamber, the surroundings had always been bizarre, intimidating, and somehow hollow. Now, Nanami was in the familiar setting of the library. In other words, her own castle.

Outside the window, snowflakes danced in the air; beyond, she could hear the joyful voices of children. Right now, Nanami was preparing to face up to this intrusion of the extraordinary into her ordinary.

"Why, indeed?" said the King, turning to look out of the window. "I don't really know myself. But you escaped so brilliantly from that fire. Perhaps I wanted to learn a little more about you."

"Somehow you also survived, even though you were in that fire too," Nanami remarked.

"I shall not perish," the King replied dismissively. "I told you before: I am the one who proliferates."

The King picked up a coin with the fingers of his left hand and placed it back on the surface of the desk with a sharp rapping sound, as if making a move in shogi.

"Let me ask you one question," he said. "How did you manage to get out of that place?"

"Is that what you're here to find out?"

The King didn't answer, instead he tapped the coin sharply on the table again.

"I know human beings very well," he announced. "They possess enormous desires and, to fulfill those desires, they are capable of displaying incredible strength. Some say that the greatest characteristic of human beings is their intellect, but they are clearly mistaken. Intelligence does indeed give rise to technology and invention. However, a truly intelligent person, despite being able to construct a gun, would never pull the trigger against a fellow human being. The act of not pulling the trigger—that is what should be termed 'intelligent.' And it's clear that humans lack that. Don't get me wrong; I don't see that as a flaw. Humans are relentless in kicking others to the ground, killing their own kind, and continuing to expand their desires. You could say that this tremendous desire is humankind's greatest weapon. It is the force that drives humans to grow, to discover, and to become greater."

Muttering to himself, he tapped the coin on the desk once more.

"But I know that even such powerful human beings can be surprisingly fragile once they are gripped by anxiety and despair. A person abandoned in a fire like that one doesn't usually survive."

"Well, it seems you've only been studying one kind of person then."

"That's always been my observation."

The King slammed the coin down onto the table. Although he remained expressionless, to Nanami's ears the sharp sound was like a scream of pain.

She was finally beginning to understand.

The King had come here in search of something. He wasn't asserting himself in the arrogant way he once did. He had come to Nanami looking for the path he should take. The King had approached this asthmatic, powerless, thirteen-year-old girl, not with contempt or a sneer, but with questions.

Nanami took a deep breath before she spoke.

"Well, I imagine that for the people you've been talking about, it would have been impossible to escape from there."

She grasped the words that floated up in her chest, almost unconsciously, and laid them out on the desk.

The King looked back at her, his expression blank.

"The people I'm talking about?"

"As you said, people who have no regard for others are certainly powerful. They can kick someone to the ground without a second thought. Those kinds of people don't worry whether what they do is wrong. But as you also commented, they are surprisingly fragile."

"Why is that?"

"Because they're all alone."

The King didn't respond.

"Because when they find themselves alone in the fire, no one will offer them a hand."

It was strange how the words came so naturally to Nanami. It wasn't logical or methodical but, through a simple desire to communicate, she found the words gently piling at her feet like snowflakes. All she had to do was bend down and carefully scoop them up.

"What I needed to escape from those flames wasn't to live more freely, or to be true to myself, or anything complicated like intellect or desire. And, of course, it wasn't a musket or a grease-covered factory, either."

"Then what was it?"

"It's hard to answer that because it's not something that can be explained in conversation."

"Are you telling me to read a book?"

The King turned his glassy stare on her.

Nanami didn't reply; she simply stared back into his eyes, not averting her gaze even for a moment.

The King remained motionless for a while, but then his gray lips moved again.

"Is that what you truly believe?"

There was no mockery or scorn in the King's voice, so Nanami gave him an honest answer.

"Books become imbued with the power of all the people who have encountered them. That power is what pulled me out of that inferno. I was just able to sense it."

"Hard to believe. The power of books leaves a person weak and helpless. Empathy, sympathy, consideration—all those kinds of emotions weaken people's resolve, take away their ability to make decisions, and also lower their levels of aggression. In other words, they diminish a person's potential and make it more difficult to succeed."

"There are more important things than success."

The King's gaze did not waver.

"I'm not saying that it isn't important to succeed," Nanami continued, "but books teach us that other things are more important. Like reaching out to help someone in need, listening to someone who is troubled, and understanding that there are things more valuable than money. They teach us ideas that can't be explained by logic alone, concepts that are perhaps not so much the norm these days, but used to be common sense. And everyone understood them. If you read a book, you'd understand immediately."

"But, as you said, so many people have already forgotten about these concepts. Doesn't that mean they're pointless nowadays? That they no longer serve any purpose?"

"Not at all. They give you great strength."

"For example?"

"They teach you that there is hope to be found in all places. That you're never alone. That you can run through a sea of flames and find your way out."

In Nanami's mind as she spoke, she saw a small field mouse bowing its head, the mischievous grin on the face of a master thief, a blue flag fluttering above a gray one, and finally an imperious-looking cat striding ahead . . .

The King lifted his eyes upward to the bare ceiling. He appeared to be listening intently to Nanami's words.

"I hear the same thing every day at school too," Nanami

went on. "'Live your life the way you want. Don't listen to other people's opinions, just express your own. And work harder and harder so you'll succeed in society.' But I believe that way of thinking is completely wrong."

Nanami placed one hand on the book in front of her.

"It's not easy at all to explain why it's wrong. Maybe it's not something you understand through logic. It's something you feel with your heart."

Nanami looked down at her book.

"That's why people read books. When they do, they can feel it, what it means to be considerate of others, what happens to those who forget how to be compassionate. And sometimes, an old, gentle book will ask, 'Do you want to be rich, or do you want to be happy?'"

"Isn't it human nature to try to be both?"

"Perhaps. But it's impossible. In every fairy tale, you have to choose between the big treasure chest or the small one."

Nanami spoke smoothly and her voice filled the deserted library. Around them it was as silent as if time had stopped.

"But, you see," the King blurted out, tapping the coin on the desk again, "I've grown too big. So big that I could blow away the fragile human heart with a single breath . . . The humans themselves can no longer control me. I've expanded into a kind of massive, bloated darkness, and I am trying to engulf humanity in my dark chaos. Do you think you would still be able to speak those words from within that darkness?"

Although he had phrased it as a question, his words were clearly meant to be rhetorical.

His gray face still lacked any expression whatsoever. No anger, no mockery.

"I have walked beside people for thousands of years."

At the moment of the King's declaration, a thick, black substance began to trickle from his feet and creep upward.

"Thousands of years . . . ?"

Nanami repeated the words in a kind of daze as the thick, oppressive darkness slowly oozed toward her shoes. She couldn't move. The eerie presence that she had felt back in the castle was spreading here in the library, bringing with it icy-cold air.

"In the beginning, I was just a seashell by the shore. No more than a beautiful pebble. Gradually, I added various adornments, changed my appearance, and infiltrated the human world, passing through the hands of many. And everyone who came into contact with me began to change. They wanted more and more of me."

Nanami could no longer hear any sounds from outside. She sat in complete darkness. All she could see was the Gray King sitting before her. Everything else had vanished.

The weight of the darkness was overwhelming; she felt the urge to scream. But Nanami pressed her lips tightly together. She was able to stand firm because she knew now that she was not alone.

Just as these thoughts ran through her head, the outline of the King sitting across from her began to blur before her eyes. The image of that tall, suited gentleman distorted, transforming into the heavily built General, then again into the slim young Prime Minister, and finally into a frail old woman with a hunched back. Although she appeared weak and helpless, a sinister aura flowed around the old woman's feet like muddy water.

"It started with small changes that gradually spread throughout the world, and now everywhere has become a great melting pot of desires. I, merely by existing, am a source of power for people. And just by existing, I continue to grow. The more of me that is gathered, the more I increase. And this drives people to want ever more of me. To get hold of more, people began to lie, cheat, harm others, and eventually, to kill."

The old woman squirmed slightly. To Nanami she looked to be writhing in pain.

"With something that is not meant to grow and yet continues to do so, this inevitably creates distortions. A person can manage a small amount of wealth. But, as is the case these days, with vast amounts continuing to multiply, huge sacrifices are required. People ignore the sacrifices being made and focus only on the increases. They call this 'growth.' This growth feeds on itself, leading to ever more bloated desire. There have been great heroes throughout history who recognized the dangers of such barbaric attitudes. They realized that wealth, too, must decay over time, or it will be out of harmony with nature. However, 'those who have much' have always quietly suppressed those voices. Of course, for them, the power of proliferation is their golden rule that promises even greater power."

The old woman's right hand fumbled in midair as if trying to grasp hold of something. It was a shockingly emaciated hand, the bones prominent beneath the skin.

"What are humans doing? Growth? It's foolishness. The idea that those who have so much and those who have so little can grow together is a pathetic illusion. As the former becomes richer, the latter becomes poorer. Wealth is not absolute; it is relative. Everyone pretends to be unaware of this, but deep down, they must know it's true. That's why they deceive and harm others, plunder from them, clinging desperately to the exclusivity that ranks them as 'winners.' What on earth are they doing? A world where the corpses of countless poor lie beneath a handful of monstrous victors. They call this horrendous barbarism 'freedom.' Read the banner. It says 'self.'"

The gray wizened woman turned her vacant eyes toward Nanami. Behind those two pinpricks lurked something immense, something that encompassed everything, a profound darkness that was spreading, ready to suck up and swallow everything in its reach.

Sweat began to form on Nanami's forehead.

She had no words to respond to the vast, overwhelming story laid out before her. She could never have anticipated confronting such a massive entity. A faint image of Rintaro flashed through her mind. Was this the reason he had hesitated and faltered, unable to find the words to respond?

"You are still a child."

The old woman's withered voice had transformed into a deep, commanding one. Nanami looked more closely and saw that the tiny, hunched shadow had turned into the formidable figure of the General.

"It must be difficult for you to understand what I'm saying," he said. "There is so much you don't know."

"And yet, even though I know nothing, you came here to speak to me . . ." replied Nanami, struggling to steady her breathing.

Once again, the silhouette before her began to blur, and this time took on the form of the Prime Minister.

"Because I found you intriguing," said the Prime Minister. "You really were aided by the power of books to escape that inferno. And if you can harness that power, perhaps you'll be able to change things."

There was something earnest in his voice, as though he was asking a genuine question.

"Sooner or later, you will come face-to-face with the vortex of desire. When that time comes, will there still be a book in your hand? Or will you, too, in the name of freedom and self be seeking more and more?"

"If that ever happens . . ."

Nanami clenched her fists and tried to shake off the chilling darkness that enveloped her.

". . . then come back again."

Her brief sentence was instantly swallowed up by the darkness.

The figure of the Prime Minister had already become fuzzy and, as Nanami watched, it wavered between the form of the General and the King, then at moments took on the appearance of a young woman or a little boy.

Nanami gathered all her strength to face up to her elusive opponent.

"If I ever change, come back here and yell at me. Tell me to get it together!"

She knew what she was saying didn't make any sense, but she couldn't find any other words to express herself. She took a deep breath and raised her voice.

"I have no idea what the future holds. Compared to you, who has seen many different things, I know nothing at all. I don't understand even half of what you're talking about. So I won't say that everything's going to be fine. Instead, I'm asking you a favor—if I ever lose my way, come back and tell me off. Put me right."

The darkness held strong.

The gray shadow before her was partially enshrouded, its current form indistinct. But Nanami could sense that someone—or something—was right beside her, listening intently.

She had no idea how much time had passed, but somehow the gray-suited King was back, sitting across from her in the darkness. And he was looking straight at her, his expression calm. It felt as if their eyes were meeting for the first time. After their long conversation, it was as if, for the first time, the Gray Man was really seeing her.

She forced herself to sound more cheery.

"I won't ever give up my books. But if I do, make sure you come and let me know. Ask me 'What do you think you're doing? You're that incredible person who made it out of a blazing castle!' You can shout at me. Tell me to get a grip."

Even though there were many things Nanami didn't grasp, there was one thing she truly understood—that no matter how strongly you believed in something, that belief could be shattered in an instant.

Her father, who had always been so kind and thoughtful, had become overwhelmed with work and lost sight of himself. Her teacher, who should have been kind and supportive, had ostracized her. And there was the time that she was relieved to have been brought to the hospital only to be met with a look of exasperation from the doctor. None of these people was deliberately malicious; it was simply that while struggling to get by they had gradually lost a little piece of their hearts.

However, losing something doesn't mean it's gone forever. If you have someone close to you, just a whispered word from them can help you to get it back.

"The most frightening thing isn't the idea of losing your heart. It's that no one will tell you you've lost it. It's having no friends to tell you you're wrong when you treat someone badly. In other words, being all alone."

Quite possibly the world was full of people who didn't even realize they were alone.

"But I'll be okay. I have lots of friends who tell me what I need to know. Precious friends like you."

The King's eyes widened ever so slightly. It was a tiny movement, but it betrayed his surprise. This was the first time the Gray Man's face had shown anything resembling an expression.

"Just in case you didn't hear me, I'll say it again," said Nanami. "You have become a friend to me. And, therefore, I'm going to say the same thing to you: Get a grip!"

The darkness didn't immediately dissipate. Instead, Nanami and the King continued to face each other in the black void. Though the King's face remained gray and expressionless, the stifling presence in the air began to lift a little.

The King shifted his gaze from Nanami to his own right hand. He raised up the coin and placed it gently on the desk. At the faint tap the gesture made, the darkness finally dispersed, and they were sitting once more in the familiar surroundings of the library.

The King remained still. Nanami also said nothing. She simply watched him as he stared at the coin on the desk. She gazed at the profile of this great being who had walked the earth for thousands of years.

Everything has a soul. Sayo's words echoed in Nanami's mind.

Yes, it was true.

It wasn't only books that had a soul. The possession of a soul wasn't limited to tangible objects, either. If human thoughts and emotions continued to gather around words, or even abstract concepts, these would eventually possess a soul and take on a life of their own. And, as Rintaro had said, *Something that has been in the hands of a person with a twisted soul will also acquire a twisted soul.*

The King had been with humans since time immemorial, traveling the world, changing form and shape, transcending even the passage of time. He had crossed vast oceans of dreadful desires.

"It's strange," the King began abruptly.

Nanami was startled, because there was no coldness in

his tone. On the contrary, there was a trace of emotion in his words.

"Every once in a while, I meet someone like you. It doesn't change anything, yet I feel something different from despair."

He took a small breath.

"Nanami," he said, looking at her.

She couldn't read his emotions, but she met his gaze head-on.

"Don't forget," he said in a deep, gentle voice. "What you see is not everything. The most important things always reside in the heart."

He got slowly to his feet, taking his cap from the desk and putting it on his head. Then he took a small object from his pocket and placed it on the desk.

"You left this behind."

Nanami gasped. It was the asthma inhaler that had slipped from her hand on the spiral staircase.

When she looked up, the gray-suited King was already walking away, having offered no words of farewell. She watched him disappear out of sight between the bookshelves.

The sound of his footsteps faded away, until there was only silence.

It was very quiet. Outside the window, a snow-coated landscape.

HOW IT ALL ENDED

On the school grounds several snowmen stood in a row. The first snowfall that winter had been rather late, and the snow, when it finally arrived, had seemed hesitant, falling only intermittently over the following days. But then, as if the weather had suddenly decided to stop dithering, it had gone all out with a proper snowstorm. The storm had picked up intensity overnight, continuing through the next day, and now the whole town was shrouded in a white haze.

The roads were just about passable, thanks to the snowplows, but the sidewalks had been left untouched. A woman in boots tottered unsteadily by the mounds of snow, an umbrella in one hand. Christmas trees that adorned the doorways of some houses were half buried by the snow, their twinkling lights creating a magical effect.

Nanami sat at the desk on the second floor of the library with an open copy of *The Moon and Sixpence* in front of her. Instead of reading, though, she stared out at the snow-covered town. According to the weather forecast, the snow was expected to stop falling by the afternoon, but this was still the heaviest snowfall in recent years. Even for Nanami, who always sat in that seat and looked out over the town, today was a rare sight.

"What are you reading?"

The voice belonged to the old librarian who was doing his rounds, wiping down the desks in the reading corner.

Nanami lifted her book slightly to show the cover.

"Ah, *The Moon and Sixpence*. Somerset Maugham's masterpiece. A good choice," he said.

"Of course it is. You're the one who recommended it to me, Hamura-san."

The old man raised an eyebrow at her reply, but didn't seem unduly bothered by it.

"Maugham is a first-rate writer, but he's also an excellent critic. He wrote a nonfiction work called *Ten Novels and Their Authors* and he certainly picked ten very fine works for his list."

"I haven't heard of that before. Please tell me about it sometime. I'd like to read it," Nanami said.

"I've already told you about it. *Wuthering Heights* is one of the books on that list," Old Ham responded in his gruff manner, although there was a hint of amusement in his tone. "When you're done reading that one, stop by the reception desk again. Just make sure it's when we're not busy."

With that, Old Ham moved on, still wiping down the desks. He may have looked grumpy, but his work was always meticulous, and he never cut corners. The old librarian's critical eye could be compared with Maugham's own. Old Ham was truly the living encyclopedia of the library.

Despite the weather, the library was unusually busy today. Perhaps the locals had nowhere else to go in the heavy snow. As Nanami watched the old man move away, she spotted her friend crossing the library floor toward her.

"Nanami, sorry I'm late!"

Itsuka waved as she hurried over. Today she wasn't carrying her usual bow but was bundled up in a heavy coat with a shoulder bag.

"It's snowing like crazy outside!" she announced.

Her short hair and the shoulders of her coat were covered in snowflakes.

"When everything turns white like that it's like some magical scene from a book," replied Nanami, slipping a bookmark into *The Moon and Sixpence*.

"You sound so nonchalant, but do you realize that at this rate the trains might stop running?"

"I hope not," said Nanami as she snapped the book shut.

Itsuka put her bag down on a nearby chair.

"Do you think you can walk in this snow?" she asked.

"Of course. I can handle it."

"You sure?"

"Yes, because I know you're dying to go to Natsuki Books too."

"Well, that's true."

Itsuka pondered for a moment.

"If we don't go, I won't get to meet the talking cat, will I?"

"What are you talking about? Cats can't talk!"

"You've betrayed me, Nanami!" joked Itsuka, as Nanami put her novel away in her bag.

The girls had already made a plan to visit Natsuki Books that day.

A Christmas party.

This was something Rintaro had suggested about a week ago, but the term was unfamiliar to Nanami. It had come up in conversation when they were chatting, and to Nanami, who was used to spending her free time alone with a book, it didn't mean much. Rintaro had laughed.

"Usually Sayo and I just enjoy a cup of tea and a slice of cake together, but this year we wondered if you'd like to join us."

That quaint old bookshop didn't really fit with the image of Christmas in Nanami's head. Sayo, who had been dusting the bookshelves, apparently read her thoughts. She turned and whispered, "Christmas Eve is a special day for Rintaro and me."

Nanami blushed at Sayo's secretive tone, without fully understanding why. Rintaro hastily interjected.

"Don't go saying weird stuff to a junior high schooler, Sayo."

"There's nothing weird about it," Sayo protested. "You have to admit it is a special day for us."

"Well, when you say special . . ."

"It *is* special. It's the day a reclusive high school student made his mind up to protect this little bookshop."

Rintaro fell silent. Sayo leaned in close to Nanami's ear and whispered, "And the day I decided I wanted to be with Rintaro."

Seeing Nanami turn an even deeper shade of red, Rintaro grew quite concerned, but Sayo was totally unbothered. When it came to topics like this, Nanami realized the deeply thoughtful Rintaro was no match for Sayo.

At some point in the conversation, Nanami had asked them if she could bring her friend Itsuka along. Of course, they agreed. After returning home, she had asked her father, who gave his permission, on the condition that he would come and pick them up by car in the evening.

And thus, a plan for an entirely new adventure was set in motion.

Nanami was restless all week. She still hadn't made sense of what had happened that day at the library with the Gray Man. There were so many things she wanted to ask Rintaro and Sayo, but she didn't know how to even begin to explain. Thinking about it made her head spin, and now, she was about to take a train with Itsuka to attend a Christmas party.

After worrying endlessly about all of it, Nanami eventually decided to stop thinking about it altogether. As Sayo had once said, time would tell. The best thing to do was probably to "relax and browse the bookshelves until the temperature was right."

"Isn't that a large bag just to go to a party?"

At Itsuka's comment, Nanami gave her bag a gentle pat.

"That's because it's full of books. There's *Solaris*, which I borrowed from here, and then there's *Vie de Beethoven* by Romain Rolland and *Sanshirō* by Natsume Sōseki that I got from Natsuki Books."

"Are you reading all three at once?"

"They're all completely different from one another. One's about a psychologist in space, one is about a composer, and the last one is about a college student. And this one, *The Moon and Sixpence*, I grabbed from the shelf just now—it's about a painter."

Itsuka looked dismayed at Nanami's animated explanation.

"Well then, once you've put the painter's story back on the bookshelf, perhaps we can get going?"

"Okay!" said Nanami cheerfully, jumping to her feet.

Nanami had a peculiar habit of reading multiple books at once, yet still feeling the need to reach for new ones. There were always so many books she wanted to read, far more than she could keep up with.

The Moon and Sixpence belonged in the British Literature section, so Nanami asked Itsuka to watch her belongings as she walked over to the back shelves. Since she'd only picked it up earlier, she knew exactly where to put it back. After returning the book to its correct place, she murmured a small "right then" to herself. She started back to her friend, but then came to a halt in front of the French Literature aisle.

Her eyes wandered down the long passageway.

What lay before her was just an ordinary aisle between the shelves. No bluish-white light, no unending rows of bookshelves. Simply a straightforward corridor with a bookcase across the end. If she reached out, she could touch the complete collection of Baudelaire's works, neatly arranged—with no odd gaps between the tightly packed books.

It was a peaceful, perfectly normal scene.

Nothing much had changed since the day she had watched the man in the gray suit walk away. Nothing had been resolved, and her perspective hadn't suddenly broadened. But something inside her had shifted, even if only a little. She'd found herself yearning to learn more.

She'd realized she knew far too little about the world. It wasn't enough to sit there in the library with an open book; she needed to walk outside on her own two feet. Eventually, she wanted to be able to understand at least half of what the Gray Man had talked about. To do that, she needed to step beyond the narrow world she had begun to shut herself away in, if only at a very gradual pace. She understood that now.

As these thoughts swirled in her mind, Nanami's gaze moved to the foot of the bookcase at the far end of the aisle.

A cat was sitting there—a tabby cat with ears the shape of isosceles triangles and eyes the color of jade. Its fur was sleek, and its silver whiskers elegant. A cat simply sitting there, exuding an air of dignity.

Nanami wasn't a bit surprised. She paused for a moment, her hand resting on the shelf, and stared back at the cat.

Then, as if it were the most natural thing in the world, she asked, "Is there something up today?"

The cat gave a small flick of its tail.

"Just my regular patrol."

That familiar deep voice . . .

"I was concerned that some troublemaker might have made off with a book again," the cat elaborated.

"Looks like everything's fine for now."

"So it does," the cat agreed.

The cat and the girl exchanged a silent glance.

Then, a little smile.

"I thought I'd never see you again . . ."

Nanami tried to keep her tone casual, but her voice trembled slightly.

"Rintaro told me that you weren't the type to return once your business was concluded."

"But I have unfinished business," replied the cat. "I still have to thank you."

"Thank me?"

"You saved me from that fire. I never got the chance to thank you for it. It was because of you that I was able to get out of that castle."

Nanami couldn't find any words to respond. It was too difficult to hold back the feelings that were welling up. She could have said something like *We helped each other* or *You really helped me too*, but the words that finally made their way out were quite different.

"After that it got pretty heavy, you know? It was a real struggle," she said with a forced smile.

The cat gave a grandiose nod.

"Indeed. It must have been terrible for you. Yet you never gave up. You ran as hard as you could and kept on going to the end. And above all, you never lost hope."

It was difficult for Nanami to maintain her smile when she listened to the warm voice of the cat. In truth, she believed that she was the one who had been saved. She hadn't given up because the cat had taught her not to. But she couldn't put that feeling into words. If she'd tried, she was certain the words would sound shallow.

She had an urge to run over and hug the cat, but she knew if she did, it would immediately turn and leave. So she stayed where she was.

"I won't ask if we'll meet again," she said.

"A wise decision. Humans are so wasteful with their words."

With that the cat slowly stood up.

"It was good to see you," said Nanami hurriedly, anxious to delay its exit.

It worked. The cat stopped for a moment and looked back at her.

"Take care of that body of yours."

"I'll be fine. So—"

Nanami broke off for a moment, then went on.

"If you're ever in trouble again, call me. I'll do some warm-up exercises so I'll be ready to go anytime."

The cat opened its jade eyes wide, then gave a small laugh. And with that, it leapt gracefully into the air like a soft breeze passing and disappeared into the shadows of the bookshelves.

All that remained were rows of ordinary, nondescript metal bookcases. There had been no time to say goodbye.

"Nanami, what's going on?"

It was Itsuka's voice across the library, worried that her friend hadn't returned.

"I'll be right there!" Nanami called back.

She looked once more down the long aisle, but of course there was no cat to be seen. With renewed determination, she addressed the empty space where it had just been.

"Call me anytime. I'll always come."

She turned around and headed back past the bookshelves to where Itsuka was waiting, bag in hand.

The snow that had been falling so heavily had somehow stopped. Sunlight was pouring through the gaps between the clouds, brightening up even the interior of the library. Outside, the town gleamed a bright shade of silver.

Nanami squinted at the dazzling view but she didn't stop moving. The crisp winter light illuminated her path.

A NOTE FROM THE COVER DESIGNER

There is always a combination of excitement, anticipation, and nervous energy at the start of any cover project, but the levels were off the charts when *The Cat Who Saved the Library* launched. The cover for *The Cat Who Saved Books* has become such an iconic visual for the HarperVia brand, so it was important for me to tap into a similar headspace for Sosuke Natsukawa's next novel.

Acclaimed illustrator Yuko Shimizu again accepted the illustration assignment and read the entire manuscript in Japanese. Her drafts were stunning, and through many conversations with her and discussions with the team, we eventually pursued a direction that combined a sketch of mine with her signature style and charm. A true creative collaborative effort.

A NOTE FROM THE COVER DESIGNER

The final piece zooms out to reveal a fuller scene with Tiger surrounded by books. Tiger's direct gaze invites you to enter the library and continue along the book-saving journey.

—Stephen Brayda

ABOUT THE AUTHOR

Sosuke Natsukawa is a Japanese physician and novelist. He graduated from the Shinshu University medical school and practices medicine at a hospital in the largely rural prefecture of Nagano. His multivolume debut novel, *Kamisama no karute* (God's medical records), has won several prizes and has sold over three million copies in Japan. *The Cat Who Saved Books* was an international bestseller. *The Cat Who Saved the Library* is the second book in the bestselling series featuring Tiger the talking tabby cat.

Louise Heal Kawai has been a Japanese-English literary translator since 2006. Her first publication was Shoko Tendo's bestselling autobiography *Yakuza Moon*. She has gone on to translate a large number of crime fiction titles, including Seishi Yokomizo's *The Honjin Murders* and *Death on Gokumon*

ABOUT THE AUTHOR

Island, as well as works by Seichō Matsumoto. Her literary translations include *Ms Ice Sandwich* by Mieko Kawakami and Hideo Yokoyama's *Seventeen*, which was longlisted for the 2019 Best Translated Book Award. She is also the translator of Sosuke Natsukawa's *The Cat Who Saved Books*. Louise comes from Manchester in the UK and currently resides in Yokohama.

Here ends Sosuke Natsukawa's
The Cat Who Saved the Library.

The first edition of this book was printed
and bound at Lakeside Book Company
in Harrisonburg, Virginia, in March 2025.

A NOTE ON THE TYPE

This novel was set in Century Schoolbook, a transitional serif typeface designed by Morris Fuller Benton in 1919. He was commissioned to create the font when Ginn & Company, a textbook publisher, approached the American Type Founders in search of an easy-to-read typeface for educational texts. Since its creation, Century Schoolbook has become synonymous with readability and has enjoyed widespread popularity, and it has been used to teach North American children how to read for generations.

HarperVia

An imprint dedicated to publishing international voices,
offering readers a chance to encounter other lives and other
points of view via the language of the imagination.